THE RAID OF THE GUERILLA

HE INSISTED THAT THEY SHOULD SHAKE HANDS AS ON A SOLEMN COMPACT

THE RAID OF THE GUERILLA
AND OTHER STORIES

by
MARY NOAILLES MURFREE
(Charles Egbert Craddock, pseud.)

With Illustrations by
W. HERBERT DUNTON AND REMINGTON SCHUYLER

Short Story Index Reprint Series

362428

 BOOKS FOR LIBRARIES PRESS
FREEPORT, NEW YORK

First Published 1912
Reprinted 1971

PS2454
.R3x
1971

INTERNATIONAL STANDARD BOOK NUMBER:
0-8369-3853-4

LIBRARY OF CONGRESS CATALOG CARD NUMBER:
71-150556

PRINTED IN THE UNITED STATES OF AMERICA

CONTENTS

	PAGE
THE RAID OF THE GUERILLA	7
WHO CROSSES STORM MOUNTAIN?	52
THE CRUCIAL MOMENT	78
UNA OF THE HILL COUNTRY	109
THE LOST GUIDON	138
WOLF'S HEAD	166
HIS UNQUIET GHOST	200
A CHILHOWEE LILY	242
THE PHANTOM OF BOGUE HOLAUBA	272
THE CHRISTMAS MIRACLE	307

ILLUSTRATIONS

	PAGE
HE INSISTED THAT THEY SHOULD SHAKE HANDS AS ON A SOLEMN COMPACT .... *Frontispiece*	
HE CAME UP LIKE A WHIRLWIND......................	30
THE UNITED WEIGHT AND IMPETUS OF THE ONSET BURST THE FLIMSY DOORS INTO FRAGMENTS...............	232
WITH ONE HAND HOLDING BACK HER DENSE YELLOW HAIR . . . SHE LOOKED UP AT HIM............	236

THE RAID OF THE GUERILLA

Judgment day was coming to Tanglefoot Cove—somewhat in advance of the expectation of the rest of the world. Immediate doom impended. A certain noted guerilla, commanding a reckless troop, had declared a stern intention of raiding this secluded nook among the Great Smoky Mountains, and its denizens could but tremble at the menace.

Few and feeble folk were they. The volunteering spirit rife in the early days of the Civil War had wrought the first depletion in the number. Then came, as time wore on, the rigors of the conscription, with an extension of the limits of age from the very young to the verge of the venerable, thus robbing, as was said, both the cradle and the grave. Now only the ancient weaklings and the frail callow remained of the male population among the women and girls, who seemed mere supernumeraries in the scheme of creation, rated by the fitness to bear arms.

So feeble a community of non-combatants might hardly compass a warlike affront cal-

THE RAID OF THE GUERILLA

culated to warrant reprisal, but the predominant Union spirit of East Tennessee was all a-pulse in the Cove, and the deed was no trifle.

" 'T war Ethelindy's deed," her grandfather mumbled, his quivering lips close to the knob of his stick, on which his palsied, veinous hands trembled as he sat in his armchair on the broad hearth of the main room in his little log cabin.

Ethelinda Brusie glanced quickly, furtively, at his pondering, wrinkled old face under the broad brim of his white wool hat, which he still wore, though indoors and with the night well advanced. Then she fixed her anxious, excited blue eyes once more on the flare of the fire.

" Lawd! ye jes' now f'und that out, dad? " exclaimed her widowed mother, busied in her evening task of carding wool on one side of the deep chimney, built of clay and sticks, and seeming always the imminent prey of destruction. But there it had stood for a hundred years, dispensing light and warmth and cheer, itself more inflammable than the great hickory logs that had summer still

THE RAID OF THE GUERILLA

among their fibres and dripped sap odorously as they sluggishly burned.

Ethelinda cast a like agitated glance on the speaker, then her gaze reverted to the fire. She had the air of being perched up, as if to escape the clutching waves of calamity, as she sat on a high, inverted splint basket, her feet not touching the puncheons of the rude floor, one hand drawing close about her the red woollen skirt of her dress. She seemed shrunken even from her normal small size, and she listened to the reproachful recital of her political activity with a shrinking dismay on her soft, roseate face.

"Nuthin' would do Ethelindy," her granny lifted an accusatory voice, still knitting briskly, though she looked rebukingly over her spectacles at the cowering girl, "when that thar Union *dee*-tachmint rid into Tanglefoot Cove like a rat into a trap——"

"Yes," interposed Mrs. Brusie, "through mistakin' it fur Greenbrier Cove."

"Nuthin' would do Ethelindy but she mus' up an' offer to show the officer the way out by that thar cave what tunnels through the spur of the mounting down todes the bluffs,

THE RAID OF THE GUERILLA

what sca'cely one o' the boys left in the Cove would know now."

"Else he'd hev been capshured," Ethelinda humbly submitted.

"Yes"—the ruffles of her grandmother's cap were terrible to view as they wagged at her with the nodding vehemence of her prelection—"an' *you* will be capshured now."

The girl visibly winced, and one of the three small boys lying about the hearth, sharing the warm flags with half a dozen dogs, whimpered aloud in sympathetic fright. The others preserved a breathless, anxious silence.

"You-uns mus' be powerful keerful ter say nuthin' 'bout Ethelindy's hand in that escape of the Fed'ral cavalry"—the old grandfather roused himself to a politic monition. "Mebbe the raiders won't find it out —an' the folks in the Cove dun 'no' who done it, nuther."

"Yes, bes' be keerful, sure," the grandame rejoined. "Fur they puts wimmin folks in jail out yander in the flat woods;" still glibly knitting, she jerked her head toward the western world outside the limits of the great ranges. "Whenst I war a gal

THE RAID OF THE GUERILLA

I war acquainted with a woman what pizened her husband, an' they kep' her in jail a consider'ble time—a senseless thing ter do, ter jail her, ter my mind, fur he war a shif'less no-'count fool, an' nobody but her would hev put up with him ez long ez she did. The jedge an' jury thunk the same, fur they 'lowed ez she war crazy—an' so she war, ter hev ever married him! They turned her loose, but she never got another husband—I never knowed a man-person but what was skittish 'bout any onhealthy meddlin' with his vittles.''

She paused to count the stitches on her needles, the big shadow of her cap-ruffles bobbing on the daubed and chinked log walls in antic mimicry, while down Ethelinda's pink cheeks the slow tears coursed at the prospect of such immurement.

'' Jes' kase I showed a stranger his path——''

'' An' two hundred an' fifty mo'—spry, good-lookin' youngsters, able to do the rebs a power o' damage.''

'' I war 'feared they'd git capshured. That man, the leader, he stopped me down on the bank o' the creek whar I war a-huntin'

THE RAID OF THE GUERILLA

of the cow, an' he axed 'bout the roads out'n the Cove. An' I tole him thar war no way out 'ceptin' by the road he had jes' come, an' a path through a sorter cave or tunnel what the creek had washed out in the spur o' the mounting, ez could be travelled whenst the channel war dry or toler'ble low. An' he axed me ter show him that underground way."

"An' ye war full willin'," said Mrs. Brusie, in irritation, "though ye knowed that thar guerilla, Ackert, hed been movin' heaven an' earth ter overhaul Tolhurst's command before they could reach the main body. An' hyar they war cotched like a rat in a trap."

"I was sure that the Cornfeds, ez hed seen them lope down inter the Cove, would be waitin' ter capshur them when they kem up the road agin—I jes' showed him how ter crope out through the cave," Ethelinda sobbed.

"How in perdition did they find thar way through that thar dark hole?—I can't sense that!" the old man suddenly mumbled.

"They had lanterns an' some pine-knots, grandad, what they lighted, an' the leader sent a squad ter 'reconnoitre,' ez he called

THE RAID OF THE GUERILLA

it. An' whilst he waited he stood an' talked ter me about the roads in Greenbrier an' the lay o' the land over thar. He war full perlite an' genteel."

"I'll be bound ye looked like a 'crazy Jane,'" cried the grandmother, with sudden exasperation. "Yer white sun-bonnet plumb off an' a-hangin' down on yer shoulders, an' yer yaller hair all a-blowsin' at loose eends, stiddier bein' plaited up stiff an' tight an' personable, an' yer face burned pink in the sun, stiddier like yer skin ginerally looks, fine an' white ez a pan o' fraish milk, an' the flabby, slinksy skirt o' that yaller calico dress 'thout no starch in it, a-flappin' an' whirlin' in the wind—shucks! I dun'no' *whut* the man could hev thought o' you-uns, dressed out that-a-way."

"He war toler'ble well pleased with me now, sure!" retorted Ethelinda, stung to a blunt self-assertion. "He keered mo' about a good-lookin' road than a good-lookin' gal then. Whenst the squad kem back an' reported the passage full safe for man an' beastis the leader tuk a purse o' money out'n his pocket an' held it out to me—though he said it 'couldn't express his thanks.' But I

THE RAID OF THE GUERILLA

held my hands behind me an' wouldn't take it. Then he called up another man an' made him open a bag, an' he snatched up my empty milk-piggin' an' poured it nigh full o' green coffee in the bean—it be skeerce ez gold an' nigh ez precious."

"An' *what* did you do with it, Ethelindy?" her mother asked, significantly—not for information, but for the renewal of discussion and to justify the repetition of rebukes. These had not been few.

"You know," the girl returned, sullenly.

"*I* do," the glib grandmother interposed. "Ye jes' gin we-uns a sniff an' a sup, an' then ye tuk the kittle that leaks an' shook the rest of the coffee beans from out yer milk-piggin inter it, an' sot out an' marched yerself through the laurel—I wonder nuthin' didn't ketch ye! howsomever naught is never in danger—an' went ter that horspital camp o' the rebels on Big Injun Mounting—small-pox horspital it is—an' gin that precious coffee away to the enemies o' yer kentry."

"Nobody comes nor goes ter that place—hell itself ain't so avoided," said Mrs. Brusie, her forehead corrugated with sudden recurrence of anxiety. "Nobody else in this

THE RAID OF THE GUERILLA

world would have resked it, 'ceptin' that headin' contrairy gal, Ethelindy Brusie."

"I never resked nuthin'," protested Ethelinda. "I stopped at the head of a bluff far off, an' hollered down ter 'em in the clearin' an' held up the kittle. An' two or three rebs war out of thar tents in the clearin'—thar be a good sight o' new graves up thar!—an' them men war hollerin' an' wavin' me away, till they seen what I war doin'; jes' settin' down the kittle an' startin' off."

She gazed meditatively into the fire, of set purpose avoiding the eyes fixed upon her, and sought to justify her course.

"I knowed ez we-uns hed got used ter doin' 'thout coffee, an' don't feel the need of it now. We-uns air well an' stout, an' live in our good home an' beside our own h'a'th-stone; an' they air sick, an' pore, an' cast out, an' I reckon they ain't ever been remembered before in gifts. An' I 'lowed the coffee, bein' onexpected an' a sorter extry, mought put some fraish heart an' hope in 'em—leastwise show 'em ez God don't 'low 'em ter be plumb furgot."

She still gazed meditatively at the fire as

THE RAID OF THE GUERILLA

if it held a scroll of her recollections, which she gradually interpreted anew. " I looked back wunst, an' one o' them rebs had sot down on a log an' war sobbin' ez ef his heart would bust. An' another of 'em war signin' at me agin an' agin, like he was drawin' a cross in the air—one pass down an' then one across—an' the other reb war jes' laffin' fur joy, and wunst in a while he yelled out: ' Blessin's on ye! Blessin's! Blessin's! ' I dun'no' how fur I hearn that sayin'. The rocks round the creek war repeatin' it, whenst I crossed the foot-bredge. I dun'no what the feller meant—mought hev been crazy."

A tricksy gust stirred at the door as if a mischievous hand twitched the latch-string, but it hung within. There was a pause. The listening children on the hearth sighed and shifted their posture; one of the hounds snored sonorously in the silence.

" Nuthin' crazy thar 'ceptin' you-uns!— one fool gal—that's all! " said her grandmother, with her knitting-needles and her spectacles glittering in the firelight. " That is a pest camp. Ye mought hev cotch the smallpox. I be lookin' fur ye ter break out with it any day. When the war is over an' the men come back to the Cove, none of 'em will so much as look at ye, with yer skin all pock-marked—fair an' fine as it is now, like a pan of fraish milk."

"But, granny, it won't be sp'ilt! The camp war too fur off—an' thar warn't a breath o' wind. I never went a-nigh 'em."

" I dun'no' how fur smallpox kin travel— an' it jes' mulls and mulls in ye afore it breaks out—don't it, S'briny?"

" Don't ax me," said Mrs. Brusie, with a worried air. " I ain't no yerb doctor, nor nurse tender, nuther. Ethelindy is beyond my understandin'."

She was beyond her own understanding, as she sat weeping slowly, silently. The aspect of those forlorn graves, that recorded the final ebbing of hope and life at the pest camp, had struck her recollection with a most poignant appeal. Strangers, wretches, dying alone, desolate outcasts, the terror of their kind, the epitome of repulsion—they were naught to her! Yet they represented humanity in its helplessness, its suffering, its isolated woe, and its great and final mystery; she felt vaguely grieved for their sake, and she gave the clay that covered them, still crude red clods with not yet a blade of grass, the fellowship of her tears.

A thrill of masculine logic stirred uneasily in the old man's disused brain. "Tell me *one* thing, Ethelindy," he said, lifting his bleared eyes as he clasped his tremulous hands more firmly on the head of his stick—"tell me this—which side air you-uns on, ennyhow, Ethelindy?"

"I'm fur the Union," said Ethelinda, still weeping, and now and then wiping her sapphire eyes with the back of her hand, hard and tanned, but small in proportion to her size. "I'm fur the Union—fust an' last an' all the time."

The old man wagged his head solemnly with a blight of forecast on his wrinkled, aged face. "That thar sayin' is goin' ter be mighty hard ter live up to whilst Jerome Ackert's critter company is a-raidin' of Tanglefoot Cove."

The presence of the "critter company" was indeed calculated to inspire a most obsequious awe. It was an expression of arbitrary power which one might ardently wish directed elsewhere. From the moment that the echoes of the Cove caught the first

THE RAID OF THE GUERILLA

elusive strain of the trumpet, infinitely sweet and clear and compelling, yet somehow ethereal, unreal, as if blown down from the daylight moon, a filmy lunar semblance in the bland blue sky, the denizens of Tanglefoot began to tremulously confer together, and to skitter like frightened rabbits from house to house. Tanglefoot Cove is some four miles long, and its average breadth is little more than a mile. On all sides the great Smoky Mountains rise about the cuplike hollow, and their dense gigantic growths of hickory and poplar, maple and gum, were aglow, red and golden, with the largesse of the generous October. The underbrush or the jungles of laurel that covered the steeps rendered outlet through the forests impracticable, and indeed the only road was invisible save for a vague line among the dense pines of a precipitous slope, where on approach it would materialize under one's feet as a wheel track on either side of a line of frosted weeds, which the infrequent passing of wagon-beds had bent and stunted, yet had not sufficed to break.

The blacksmith's shop, the centre of the primitive civilization, had soon an expectant group in its widely flaring doors, for the smith had had enough of the war, and had come back to wistfully, hopelessly haunt his anvil like some uneasy ghost visiting familiar scenes in which he no more bears a part;— a minié-ball had shattered his stanch hammer-arm, and his duties were now merely advisory to a clumsy apprentice. This was a half-witted fellow, a giant in strength, but not to be trusted with firearms. In these days of makeweights his utility had been discovered, and now with the smith's hammer in his hand he joined the group, his bulging eyes all a-stare and his loose lips hanging apart. The old justice of the peace, whose office was a sinecure, since the war had run the law out of the Cove, came with a punctilious step, though with a sense of futility and abated dignity, and at every successive note of the distant trumpet these wights experienced a tense bracing of the nerves to await helplessly the inevitable and, alas! the inexorable.

"They say that he is a turrible, turrible man," the blacksmith averred, ever and anon rubbing the stump of his amputated hammer-arm, in which, though bundled in its jeans

THE RAID OF THE GUERILLA

sleeve, he had the illusion of the sensation of its hand and fingers. He suddenly shaded his brow with his broad palm to eye that significant line which marked the road among the pines on the eastern slope, beyond the Indian corn that stood tall and rank of growth in the rich bottom-lands.

Ethelinda's heart sank. All unprescient of the day's impending event, she had come to the forge with the sley of her loom to be mended, and she now stood holding the long shaft in her mechanical clasp, while she listened spell-bound to the agitated talk of the group. The boughs of a great yellow hickory waved above her head; near by was the trough, and here a horse, brought to be shod, was utilizing the interval by a draught; he had ceased to draw in the clear, cold spring water, but still stood with his muzzle close to the surface, his lips dripping, gazing with unimagined thoughts at the reflection of his big equine eyes, the blue sky inverted, the dappling yellow leaves, more golden even than the sunshine, and the glimmering flight of birds, with a stellular light upon their wings.

"A turrible man?—w-w-well," stuttered the idiot, who had of late assumed all the

THE RAID OF THE GUERILLA

port of coherence; he snatched and held a part in the colloquy, so did the dignity of labor annul the realization of his infirmity, "then I'd be obleeged ter him ef—ef—ef he'd stay out'n Tanglefoot Cove."

" So would I." The miller laughed uneasily. But for the corrugations of time, one might not have known if it were flour or age that had so whitened his long beard, which hung quivering down over the breast of his jeans coat, of an indeterminate hue under its frosting from the hopper. " He hev tuk up a turrible spite at Tanglefoot Cove."

The blacksmith nodded. " They say that he 'lowed ez traitors orter be treated like traitors. But *I* be a-goin' ter tell him that the Confederacy hev got one arm off'n me more'n its entitled to, an' I'm willin' ter call it quits at that."

" 'Tain't goin' ter do him no good ter raid the Cove," an ancient farmer averred; " an' it's agin' the rebel rule, ennyhows, ter devastate the kentry they live off'n—it's like sawin' off the bough ye air sittin' on." His eyes dwelt with a fearful affection on the laden fields; his old stoop-shouldered back had bent yet more under the toil that had brought his crop to this perfection, with the aid of the children whose labor was scarcely worth the strenuosity requisite to control their callow wiles.

"Shucks! He's a guerilla—he is!" retorted the blacksmith. "Accountable ter nobody! Hyar ter-day an' thar ter-morrer. Rides light. Two leetle Parrott guns is the most weight he carries."

The idiot's eyes began to widen with slow and baffled speculation. "Whut—w-whut ails him ter take arter Tangle-foot? W-w—" his great loose lips trembled with unformed words as he gazed his eager inquiry from one to another. Under normal circumstances it would have remained contemptuously unanswered, but in these days in Tanglefoot Cove a man, though a simpleton, was yet a man, and inherently commanded respect.

"A bird o' the air mus' hev carried the matter that Tolhurst's troops hed rid inter Tanglefoot Cove by mistake fur Greenbrier, whar they war ter cross ter jine the Fed'rals nigh the Cohuttas. An' that guerilla, Ackert, hed been ridin' a hundred mile at a hand-gallop ter overhaul him, an' knowin'

THE RAID OF THE GUERILLA

thar warn't but one outlet to Tanglefoot Cove, he expected ter capshur the Feds as they kem out agin. So he sot himself ter ambush Tolhurst, an' waited fur him up thar amongst the pines an' the laurel—an' he *waited*—an' *waited!* But Tolhurst never came! So whenst the guerilla war sure he hed escaped by ways unknownst he set out ter race him down ter the Cohutty Mountings. But Tolhurst had j'ined the main body o' the Federal Army, an' now Ackert is showing a clean pair o' heels comin' back. But he be goin' ter take time ter raid the Cove—his hurry will wait fur that! Somebody in Tanglefoot—the Lord only knows who—showed Tolhurst that underground way out ter Greenbrier Cove, through a sorter cave or tunnel in the mountings."

"Now — now — neighbor — *that's* guess-work," remonstrated the miller, in behalf of Tanglefoot Cove repudiating the responsibility. Perhaps the semi-mercantile occupation of measuring toll sharpens the faculties beyond natural endowments, and he began to perceive a certain connection between cause and effect inimical to personal interest.

THE RAID OF THE GUERILLA

" Waal, that is the way they went, sartain sure," protested the blacksmith. " I tracked 'em, the ground bein' moist, kase I wanted ter view the marks o' their horses' hoofs. They hev got some powerful triflin' blacksmiths in the army—farriers, they call 'em. I los' the trail amongst the rocks an' ledges down todes the cave—though it's more like one o' them tunnels we-uns used ter go through in the railroads in the army, but this one was never made with hands; jes' hollowed out by Sinking Creek. So I got Jube thar ter crope through, an' view ef thar war any hoofmarks on t'other side whar the cave opens out in Greenbrier Cove."

" An' a body would think fur sure ez the armies o' hell had been spewed out'n that black hole," said a lean man whom the glance of the blacksmith had indicated as Jube, and who spoke in the intervals of a racking cough that seemed as if it might dislocate his bones in its violence. " Hoofmarks hyar—hoofmarks thar— as if they didn't rightly know which way ter go in the marshy ground 'bout Sinking Creek. But at last they 'peared ter git tergether, an' off they tracked ter the

THE RAID OF THE GUERILLA

west————" A paroxysm of coughs intervened, and the attention of the group failed to follow the words that they interspersed.

"They tuk a short cut through the Cove —they warn't in it a haffen hour," stipulated the prudent miller. " They came an' went like a flash. Nobody seen 'em 'cept the Brusies, kase they went by thar house—an' ef they hed hed a guide, old Randal Brusie would hev named it."

" Ackert 'lows he'll hang the guide ef he ketches him," said the blacksmith, in a tone of awe. " Leastwise that's the word that's 'goin'."

Poor Ethelinda! The clutch of cold horror about her heart seemed to stop its pulsations for a moment. She saw the still mountains whirl about the horizon as if in some weird bewitchment. Her nerveless hands loosened their clasp upon the sley and it fell to the ground, clattering on the protruding roots of the trees. The sound attracted the miller's attention. He fixed his eyes warily upon her, a sudden thought looking out from their network of wrinkles.

" You didn't see no guide whenst they slipped past you-uns' house, did ye? "

THE RAID OF THE GUERILLA

Poor, unwilling casuist! She had an instinct for the truth in its purest sense, the innate impulse toward the verities unspoiled by the taint of sophistication. Perhaps in the restricted conditions of her life she had never before had adequate temptation to a subterfuge. Even now, consciously reddening, her eyes drooping before the combined gaze of her little world, she had an inward protest of the literal exactness of her phrase.

"Naw sir—I never seen thar guide."

"Thar now, what did I tell you!" the miller exclaimed, triumphantly.

The blacksmith seemed convinced. "Mought hev hed a map," he speculated. "Them fellers in the army *do* hev maps. I f'und that out whenst I war in the service."

The group listened respectfully. The blacksmith's practical knowledge of the art of war had given him the prestige of a military authority. Doubtless some of the acquiescent wights entertained a vague wonder how the army contrived to fare onward bereft of his advice. And, indeed, despite his maimed estate, his heart was the stoutest that thrilled to the iteration of the trumpet.

THE RAID OF THE GUERILLA

Nearer now it was, and once more echoing down the sunset glen.

"Right wheel, trot—*march*," he muttered, interpreting the sound of the horses' hoofs. "It's a critter company, fur sure!"

There was no splendor of pageant in the raid of the guerilla into the Cove. The pines closing above the cleft in the woods masked the entrance of the "critter company." Once a gleam of scarlet from the guidon flashed on the sight. And again a detached horseman was visible in a barren interval, reining in his steed on the almost vertical slant, looking the centaur in literal presentation. The dull thud of hoofs made itself felt as a continuous undertone to the clatter of stirrup and sabre, and now and again rose the stirring mandate of the trumpet, with that majestic, sweet sweep of sound which so thrills the senses. They were coming indubitably, the troop of the dreaded guerilla—indeed, they were already here. For while the sun still glinted on carbine and sabre among the scarlet and golden tints of the deciduous growths and the sombre green of the pines on the loftier slopes, the vanguard in column of fours were among the gray shadows at the mountains' base and speeding into the Cove at a hand-gallop, for the roads were fairly good when once the level was reached. Though so military a presentment, for they were all veterans in the service, despite the youth of many, they were not in uniform. Some wore the brown jeans of the region, girt with sword-belt and canteen, with great spurs and cavalry boots, and broad-brimmed hats, which now and again flaunted cords or feathers. Others had attained the Confederate gray, occasionally accented with a glimmer of gold where a shoulder-strap or a chevron graced the garb. And yet there was a certain homogeneity in their aspect. All rode after the manner of the section, with the " long stirrup " at the extreme length of the limb, and the immovable pose in the saddle, the man being absolutely stationary, while the horse bounded at agile speed. There was the similarity of facial expression, in infinite dissimilarity of feature, which marks a common sentiment, origin, and habitat. Then, too, they shared something recklessly haphazard, gay, defiantly dangerous, that, elusive as it might be to describe, was as definitely perceived

THE RAID OF THE GUERILLA

as the guidon, riding apart at the left, the long lance of his pennant planted on his stirrup, bearing himself with a certain stately pride of port, distinctly official.

The whole effect was concentrated in the face of the leader, obviously the inspiration of the organization, the vital spark by which it lived; a fierce face, intent, commanding. It was burned to a brick-red, and had an aquiline nose and a keen gray-green eagle-like eye; on either side auburn hair, thick and slightly curling, hung, after the fashion of the time, to his coat collar. And this collar and his shoulders were decorated with gold lace and the insignia of rank; the uniform was of fine Confederate gray, which seemed to contradict the general impression that he was but a free-lance or a bushwhacker and operated on his own responsibility. The impression increased the terror his name excited throughout the countryside with his high-handed and eccentric methods of warfare, and perhaps he would not have resented it if he were cognizant of its general acceptance.

It was a look calculated to inspire awe which he flung upon the cowering figures be-

HE CAME UP LIKE A WHIRLWIND

THE RAID OF THE GUERILLA

fore the door of the forge as he suddenly perceived them; and detaching himself from the advancing troop, he spurred his horse toward them. He came up like a whirlwind. That impetuous gallop could scarcely have carried his charger over the building itself, yet there is nothing so overwhelming to the nerves as the approaching rush of a speedy horse, and the group flattened themselves against the wall; but he drew rein before he reached the door, and whirling in the saddle, with one hand on the horse's back, he demanded:

"Where is he? Bring him out!" as if all the world knew the object of his search and the righteous reason of his enmity. "Bring him out! I'll have a drumhead court martial—and he'll swing before sunset!"

"Good evenin', Cap'n," the old miller sought what influence might appertain to polite address and the social graces.

"Evenin' be damned!" cried Ackert, angrily. "If you folks in the coves want the immunity of non-combatants, by Gawd! you gotter preserve the neutrality of non-combatants!"

"Yessir—that's reason—that's jestice,"

said the old squire, hastily, whose capacities of ratiocination had been cultivated by the exercise of the judicial functions of his modest *piepoudre* court.

Ackert unwillingly cast his eagle eye down upon the cringing old man, as if he would rather welcome contradiction than assent.

"It's accordin' to the articles o' war and the law of nations," he averred. "People take advantage of age and disability"—he glanced at the blacksmith, whose left hand mechanically grasped the stump of his right arm—"as if that could protect 'em in acts o' treason an' treachery;" then with a blast of impatience, "Where's the man?"

To remonstrate with a whirlwind, to explain to a flash of lightning, to soothe and propitiate the fury of a conflagration—the task before the primitive and inexpert Cove-dwellers seemed to partake of this nature.

"Cap'n—ef ye'd listen ter what I gotter say," began the miller.

"I'll listen arterward!" exclaimed Ackert, in his clarion voice. He had never heard of Jedburgh justice, but he had all the sentiment of that famous tribunal who

THE RAID OF THE GUERILLA

hanged the prisoners first and tried them afterward.

"Cap'n," remonstrated the blacksmith, breaking in with hot haste, hurried by the commander's gusts of impatience, forgetful that he had no need to be precipitate, since he could not produce the recusant if he would. "Cap'n—Cap'n — bear with us — we-uns don't know!"

Ackert stared in snorting amaze, a flush of anger dyeing his red cheeks a yet deeper red. Of all the subterfuges that he had expected, he had never divined this. He shifted front face in his saddle, placed his gauntleted right hand on his right side, and held his head erect, looking over the wide, rich expanse of the Cove, the corn in the field, and the fodder in the shock set amid the barbaric splendors of the wooded autumn mountains glowing in the sunset above. He seemed scenting his vengeance with some keen sense as he looked, his thin nostrils dilating as sensitively as the nostrils of his high-couraged charger now throwing up his head to sniff the air, now bending it down as he pawed the ground.

"Well, gentlemen, you have got a mighty

pretty piece o' country here, and good crops, too—which is a credit to you, seeing that the conscription has in and about drafted all the able-bodied mountaineers that wouldn't volunteer—damn 'em! But I swear by the right hand of Jehovah, I'll burn every cabin in the Cove an' every blade o' forage in the fields if you don't produce the man who guided Tolhurst's cavalry out'n the trap I'd chased 'em into, or give me a true and satisfactory account of him." He raised his gauntleted right hand and shook it in the air. "So help me God!"

There was all the solemnity of intention vibrating in this fierce asseveration, and it brought the aged non-combatants forward in eager protestation. The old justice made as if to catch at the bridle rein, then desisted. A certain *noli me tangere* influence about the fierce guerilla affected even supplication, and the "Squair" resorted to logic as the more potent weapon of the two.

"Cap'n, Cap'n," he urged, with a tremulous, aged jaw, " be pleased to consider my words. I'm a magistrate sir, or I was before the war run the law clean out o' the kentry. We dun'no' the guide—we never

THE RAID OF THE GUERILLA

seen the troops." Then, in reply to an impatient snort of negation: " If ye'll cast yer eye on the lay of the land, ye'll view how it happened. Thar's the road "—he waved his hand toward that vague indentation in the foliage that marked the descent into the vale—" an' down this e-end o' the Cove thar's nex' ter nobody livin'."

The spirited equestrian figure was standing as still as a statue; only the movement of the full pupils of his eyes, the dilation of the nostrils, showed how nearly the matter touched his tense nerves.

" Some folks in the upper e-end of the Cove 'lowed afterward they hearn a hawn; some folks spoke of a shakin' of the ground like the trompin' of horses—but them troops mus' hev passed from the foot o' the mounting acrost the aidge of the Cove."

" Scant haffen mile," put in the blacksmith, " down to a sort of cave, or tunnel, that runs under the mounting—yander—that lets 'em out into Greenbrier Cove."

"Gawd!" exclaimed the guerilla, striking his breast with his clenched, gauntleted hand as his eyes followed with the vivacity of actual sight the course of the march of the

THE RAID OF THE GUERILLA

squadron of horse to the point of their triumphant vanishment. Despite the vehemence of the phrase the intonation was a very bleat of desperation. For it was a rich and rare opportunity thus wrested from him by an untoward fate. In all the chaotic chances of the Civil War he could hardly hope for its repetition. It was part of a crack body of regulars—Tolhurst's squadron—that he had contrived to drive into this trap, this *cul-de-sac,* surrounded by the infinite fastnesses of the Great Smoky Mountains. It had been a running fight, for Tolhurst had orders, as Ackert had found means of knowing, to join the main body without delay, and his chief aim was to shake off this persistent pursuit with which a far inferior force had harassed his march. But for his fortuitous discovery of the underground exit from the basin of Tanglefoot Cove, Ackert, ambushed without, would have encountered and defeated the regulars in detail as they clambered in detachments up the unaccustomed steeps of the mountain road, the woods elsewhere being almost impassable jungles of laurel.

Success would have meant more to Ac-

THE RAID OF THE GUERILLA

kert than the value of the service to the cause, than the tumultuous afflatus of victory, than the spirit of strife to the born soldier. There had been kindled in his heart a great and fiery ambition; he was one of the examples of an untaught military genius of which the Civil War elicited a few notable and amazing instances. There had been naught in his career heretofore to suggest this unaccountable gift, to foster its development. He was the son of a small farmer, only moderately well-to-do; he had the very limited education which a restricted and remote rural region afforded its youth; he had entered the Confederate army as a private soldier, with no sense of special fitness, no expectation of personal advancement, only carried on the wave of popular enthusiasm. But from the beginning his quality had been felt; he had risen from grade to grade, and now with a detached body of horse and flying artillery his exploits were beginning to attract the attention of corps commanders on both sides, to the gratulation of friends and the growing respect of foes. He seemed endowed with the wings of the wind; to-day he was tearing up railroad tracks in the lowlands to impede the reinforcements of an army; to-morrow the force sent with the express intention of placing a period to those mischievous activities heard of his feats in burning bridges and cutting trestles in remote sections of the mountains. The probabilities could keep no terms with him, and he baffled prophecy. He had a quick invention—a talent for expedients. He appeared suddenly when least expected and where his presence seemed impossible. He had a gift of military intuition. He seemed to know the enemy's plans before they were matured; and ere a move was made to put them into execution he was on the ground with troublous obstacles to forestall the event in its very inception. He maintained a discipline to many commanders impossible. His troops had a unity of spirit that might well animate an individual. They endured long fasts, made wonderful forced marches on occasion—all day in the saddle and nodding to the pommel all night; it was even said they fought to such exhaustion that when dismounted the front rank, lying in line of battle prone upon the ground, would fall asleep between volleys, and that the second

THE RAID OF THE GUERILLA

rank, kneeling to fire above them, had orders to stir them with their carbines to insure regularity of the musketry. He had the humbler yet even more necessary equipment for military success. He could forage his troops in barren opportunities; they somehow kept clothed and armed at the minimum of expense. Did he lack ammunition—he made shift to capture a supply for his little Parrott guns that barked like fierce dogs at the rear-guard of an enemy or protected his own retreat when it jumped with his plans to compass a speedy withdrawal himself. His horses were well groomed, well fed, fine travellers, and many showed the brand U.S., for he could mount his troop when need required from the corrals of an unsuspecting encampment. He was the ideal guerilla, of infinite service to his faction in small, significant operations of disproportioned importance.

What wonder that his name was rife in rumors which flew about the country; that soon it was not only " the grapevine telegraph " that vibrated with the sound, but he was mentioned in official despatches; nay, on one signal occasion the importance of his

THE RAID OF THE GUERILLA

dashing exploit was recognized by the commander of the Army Corps in a general order published to specially commend it. Naturally his spirit rose to meet these expanding liberties of achievement. He looked for further promotion—for eminence. In a vague glimmer, growing ever stronger and clearer, he could see himself in the astral splendor of the official stars of a major-general—for in the far day of the anticipated success of the Confederacy he looked to be an officer of the line.

And now suddenly this light was dimmed; his laurels were wilting. What prestige would the capture of Tolhurst have conferred! Never had a golden opportunity like this been lost—by what uncovenanted chance had Tolhurst escaped?

"He must have had a guide! Right here in the Cove!" Ackert exclaimed. "Nobody outside would know a hole in the ground, a cave, a water-gap, a tunnel like that! Where's the man?"

"Naw, sir—naw, Cap'n! Nobody viewed the troop but one gal person an' she 'lowed she never seen no guide."

THE RAID OF THE GUERILLA

The charger whirled under the touch of the hand on the rein, and Ackert's eyes scanned with a searching intentness the group.

"Where's this girl—you?"

As the old squire with most unwelcome officiousness seized Ethelinda's arm and hurried her forward, her heart sank within her. For one moment the guerilla's fiery, piercing eyes dwelt upon her as she stood looking on, her delicately white face grown deathly pallid, her golden hair frivolously blowsed in the wind, which tossed the full skirts of her lilac-hued calico gown till she seemed poised on the very wings of flight. Her sapphire eyes, bluer than ever azure skies could seem, sought to gaze upward, but ever and anon their long-lashed lids fluttered and fell.

He was quick of perception.

"*You* have no call to be afraid," he remarked—a sort of gruff upbraiding, as if her evident trepidation impugned his justice in reprisal. "Come, you can guide me. Show me just where they came in, and just where they got out— damn 'em!"

She could scarcely control her terror when

THE RAID OF THE GUERILLA

she saw that he intended her to ride with him to the spot, yet she feared even more to draw back, to refuse. He held out one great spurred boot. Her little low-cut shoe looked tiny upon it as she stepped up. He swung her to the saddle behind him, and the great warhorse sprang forward so suddenly, with such long, swift strides, that she swayed precariously for a moment and was glad to catch the guerilla's belt—to seize, too, with an agitated clutch, his right gauntlet that he held backward against his side. His fingers promptly closed with a reassuring grasp on hers, and thus skimming the red sunset-tide they left behind them the staring group about the blacksmith shop, which the cavalrymen had now approached, watering their horses at the trough and lifting the saddles to rest the animals from the constriction of the pressure of the girths.

Soon the guerilla and the girl disappeared in the distance; the fences flew by; the shocks of corn seemed all a-trooping down the fields; the evening star in the red haze above the purple western mountains had spread its invisible pinions, and was a-wing

THE RAID OF THE GUERILLA

above their heads. Presently the heavy shadows of the looming wooded range, darkening now, showing only blurred effects of red and brown and orange, fell upon them, and the guerilla checked the pace, for the horse was among boulders and rough ledges that betokened the dry bed of a stream. Great crags had begun to line the way, first only on one marge of the channel; then the cliftybanks appeared on the other side, and at length a deep, black-arched opening yawned beneath the mountains, glooming with sepulchral shadows; in the silence one might hear drops trickling vaguely and the sudden hooting of an owl from within.

He drew up his horse abruptly, and contemplated the grim aperture.

"So they came into Tanglefoot down the road, and went out of the Cove by this tunnel?"

"Yessir!" she piped. What had befallen her voice? what appalled eerie squeak was this! She cleared her throat timorously. "They couldn't hev done it later in the fall season. Tanglefoot Creek gits ter runnin' with the fust rains."

"An' Tolhurst knew that too! He must have had a guide—a guide that knows the Cove like I know the palm of my hand! Well, I'll catch him yet, sometime. I'll hang him! I'll hang him—if I have to grow a tree a-purpose."

What strange influence had betided the landscape? Around and around circled the great stationary mountains anchored in the foundations of the earth. It was a long moment before they were still again—perhaps, indeed, it was the necessity of guarding her balance on the fiery steed, a new cause of apprehension, that paradoxically steadied Ethelinda's nerves. Ackert had dismounted, throwing the reins over his arm. He had caught sight of the hoofmarks along the moist sandy spaces of the channel, mute witness in point of number, and a guaranty of the truth of her story. A sudden glitter arrested his eyes. He stooped and picked up a broken belt-buckle with the significant initials U.S. yet showing upon it.

"I'll hang that guide yet," he muttered, his eyes dark with angry conviction, his face lowering with fury. "I'll hang him—I won't expect to prove it p'int blank. Jes' let

THE RAID OF THE GUERILLA

me git a mite o' suspicion, an' I'll guarantee the slipknot!"

She could never understand her motive, her choice of the moment.

"Cap'n Ackert," she trembled forth. There was so much significance in her tone that, standing at her side, he looked up in sudden expectation. "I tole ye the truth whenst I say I *seen* no guide"—he made a gesture of impatience; he had no time for twice-told tales—"kase—kase the guide war —war—myself."

The clear twilight fell full on his amazed, upturned face and the storm of fury it concentrated.

"What did you do it fur?" he thundered, "you limb o' perdition!"

"Jes' ter help him some. He—he—he —would hev been capshured."

He would indeed! The guerilla was very terrible to look upon as his brow corrugated, and his upturned eyes, with the light of the sky within them, flashed ominously.

"You little she-devil!" he cried, and then speech seemed to fail him.

She had begun to shiver and shed tears and emit little gusts of quaking sobs.

THE RAID OF THE GUERILLA

"Oh, I be so feared——" she whimpered. "But—but—you mustn't hang—*nobody else* on s'picion!"

There was a vague change in the expression of his face. He still stood beside the saddle, with the reins over his arm, while the horse threw his head almost to the ground and again tossed it aloft in his impatient weariness of the delay.

"An' now you are captured yourself," he said, sternly. "You are accountable fur your actions."

She burst into a paroxysm of sobs. "I never went ter tell! I meant ter keep the secret! The folks in the Cove dun'no' nuthin'. But—oh, ye *mustn't* s'picion nobody else— ye *mustn't* hang nobody else!"

Once more that indescribable change upon his face.

"You showed him the way to this pass yourself? Tell the truth!"

"He war ridin' his horse-critter—'tain't ez fast, nor fine, nor fat ez yourn."

He stroked the glossy mane with a sort of mechanical pride.

"And so he went plumb through the cave?"

THE RAID OF THE GUERILLA

" An' all the troop—they kindled pine-knots fur torches."

He glanced about him at the convenient growths.

" And they came out all safe in Greenbrier? " He winced. How the lost opportunity hurt him!

" Yessir. In Greenbrier Cove."

"Did he pay you in gold? " sneered Ackert. " Or in greenbacks? Or mebbe in Cornfed money? "

" I wouldn't hev his gold." She drew herself up proudly, though the tears were still coursing down her cheeks. " So he gin me a present—a whole passel o' coffee in my milk-piggin." Then to complete a candid confession she detailed the disposition she had made of this rare and precious luxury at the rebel smallpox camp.

His eyes seemed to dilate as they gazed up at her. " Jesus Gawd! " he exclaimed, with uncouth profanity. But the phrase was unfamiliar to her, and she caught at it with a meaning all her own.

" That's jes' it! Folks in gineral don't think o' *them,* 'cept ter git out o' thar way; an' nobody keers fur *them,* but kase Jesus *is*

THE RAID OF THE GUERILLA

Gawd He makes *somebody* remember them wunst in a while! An' they did seem passable glad."

A vague sweet fragrance was on the vesperal air; some subtle distillation of asters or jewel-weed or "mountain-snow," and the leafage of crimson sumac and purple sweet-gum and yellow hickory and the late ripening frost-grapes—all in the culmination of autumnal perfection; more than one star gleamed whitely palpitant in a sky that was yet blue and roseate with a reminiscence of sunset; a restful sentiment, a brief truce stilled the guerilla's tempestuous pulse as he continued to stand beside his horse's head while the girl waited, seated on the saddle blanket.

Suddenly he spoke to an unexpected intent. " Ye took a power o' risk in goin' nigh that Confederate pest-camp—an' yit ye're fur the Union an' saved a squadron from capture!" he upbraided the inconsistency in a soft incidental drawl.

" Yes, I be fur the Union," she trembled forth the dread avowal. " But somehows I can't keep from holpin' any I kin.

THE RAID OF THE GUERILLA

They war rebs—an' it war Yankee coffee—an' I dun'no'—I jes' dun'no'——"

As she hesitated he looked long at her with that untranslated gaze. Then he fell ponderingly silent.

Perhaps the revelation of the sanctities of a sweet humanity for a holy sake, blessing and blessed, had illumined his path, had lifted his eyes, had wrought a change in his moral atmosphere spiritually suffusive, potent, revivifying, complete. " She is as good as the saints in the Bible—an' plumb beautiful besides," he muttered beneath his fierce mustachios.

Once more he gazed wonderingly at her.

"I expect to do some courtin' in this kentry when the war is over," the guerilla said, soberly, reaching down to readjust the reins. " I haven't got time now. Will *you* be waiting fur me here in Tanglefoot Cove—if I promise not to hang you fur your misdeeds right off now? " He glanced up with a sudden arch jocularity.

She burst out laughing gleefuly in the tumult of her joyous reassurance, as she laid her tremulous fingers in his big gauntlet when

THE RAID OF THE GUERILLA

he insisted that they should shake hands as on a solemn compact. Forthwith he mounted again, and the great charger galloped back, carrying double, in the red afterglow of the sunset, to the waiting group before the flaring doors of the forge.

The fine flower of romance had blossomed incongruously in that eager heart in those fierce moments of the bitterness of defeat. Life suddenly had a new meaning, a fair and fragrant promise, and often and again he looked over his shoulder at the receding scene when the trumpets sang " to horse," and in the light of the moon the guerilla rode out of Tanglefoot Cove.

But Ethelinda saw him never again. All the storms of fate overwhelmed the Confederacy with many a rootless hope and many a plan and pride. In lieu of the materialization of the stalwart ambition of distinction that had come to dominate his life, responsive to the discovery of his peculiar and inherent gifts, his destiny was chronicled in scarce a line of the printed details of a day freighted with the monstrous disaster of a great battle; in common with others of the " missing " his bones were picked by the vultures till shoved

THE RAID OF THE GUERILLA

into a trench, where a monument rises to-day to commemorate an event and not a commander. Nevertheless, for many years the flare of the first red leaves in the cleft among the pines on the eastern slope of Tanglefoot Cove brought to Ethelinda's mind the gay flutter of the guidon, and in certain sonorous blasts of the mountain wind she could hear martial echoes of the trumpets of the guerilla.

WHO CROSSES STORM MOUNTAIN?

The wind stirred in the weighted pines; the snow lay on the ground. Here and there on its smooth, white expanse footprints betokened the woodland gentry abroad. In the pallid glister of the moon, even amid the sparse, bluish shadows of the leafless trees, one might discriminate the impression of the pronged claw of the wild turkey, the short, swift paces of the mink, the padded, doglike paw of the wolf. A progress of a yet more ravening suggestion was intimated in great hoof-marks leading to the door of a little log cabin all a-crouch in the grim grip of winter and loneliness and poverty on the slope of the mountain, among heavy, outcropping ledges of rock and beetling, overhanging crags. With icy ranges all around as far as the eye could reach, with the vast, instarred, dark sky above, it might seem as if sorrow, the world, the law could hardly take account of so slight a thing, so remote. But smoke was slowly stealing up from its stick-and-clay chimney, and its clapboarded roof sheltered a

WHO CROSSES STORM MOUNTAIN?

group with scarcely the heart to mend the fire.

Two women shivered on the broad hearth before the dispirited embers. One had wept so profusely that she had much ado to find a dry spot in her blue-checked apron, thrown over her head, wherewith to mop her tears. The other, much younger, her fair face reddened, her blue eyes swollen, her auburn curling hair all tangled on her shoulders, her voice half-choked with sobs, addressed herself to the narration of their woes, her cold, listless hands clasped about her knees as she sat on an inverted bushel-basket, for there was not a whole chair in the room.

"An' then he jes' tuk an' leveled!" she faltered.

A young hunter standing on the threshold, leaning on his rifle, a brace of wild turkeys hanging over his shoulders, half a dozen rabbits dangling from his belt, stared at her through the dull, red glow of the fading fire in amazed agitation.

"What did he level, Medory—a gun?"

"Wuss'n that!" replied the younger woman. "He leveled the weepon o' the law!"

WHO CROSSES STORM MOUNTAIN?

The man turned to look again at the curious disarray of the room. "The law don't allow him to do sech ez this!" he blurted out in rising anger. "Why, everything hyar is bodaciously broke an' busted! War it the sheriff himself ez levied?"

"'Twar jes' the dep'ty critter, Clem Tweed," explained Medora, "mighty jokified, an' he 'peared ter be middlin' drunk, an' though he said su'thin' 'bout exemptions he 'lowed ez we-uns lived at the eend o' the world."

Her mother-in-law suddenly lowered the apron from her face.

"'The jumpin'-off place,' war what Clem Tweed called it!" she interpolated with a fiery eye of indignant reminiscence.

"He did! He did!" Medora bitterly resented this fling at the remoteness of their poor home. "An' he said whilst hyar he'd level on everything in sight, ez he hoped never ter travel sech roads agin—everything in sight, even the baby an' the cat!"

"Shucks, Medory, ye know the dep'ty man war funnin' whenst he said that about the baby an' the cat! Ye know ez Clem ad-

WHO CROSSES STORM MOUNTAIN?

mitted he hed Christmas in his bones!" the elder objected.

"Waal, war Clem Tweed funnin' whenst he done sech ez that, in levyin' an execution?" Bruce Gilhooley pointed with his ramrod at the wreck of the furniture.

The two women burst into lugubrious sobs and rocked themselves back and forth in unison. "'Twar *Dad!*" Medora moaned, in smothered accents.

A pause of bewilderment ensued. Then the young man's face took on an expression of dismay so ominous that Medora's tears were checked in the ghastly fear of disasters yet to come to her father-in-law. Now and again she glanced anxiously over her shoulder at an oblong black aperture in the dusk which betokened the open door of the shed-room. Some one lurked there, evidently cherishing all aloof a grief, an anger, a despair too poignant to share.

"Dad warn't hyar whenst the dep'ty leveled," she said. "An' mighty glad we war—kase somebody mought hev got hurt. But whenst Dad kem home an' larnt the news he jes'—he jes'—he jes' lept about like a painter."

WHO CROSSES STORM MOUNTAIN?

"He did! He did!" asseverated a voice from the veiled head, all muffled in the checked apron.

"Dad 'lowed," continued Medora, "ez Peter Petrie hev persecuted and druv him ter the wall. Fust he tricked Dad out'n some unoccupied lan' what Dad hed begun ter clear, an' Petrie got it entered fust an' tuk out a grant an' holds the title! An' whenst Dad lay claim ter it Peter Petrie declared ef enny Gilhooley dared ter cross Storm Mounting he'd break every bone in his body!"

"A true word—the insurance of the critter!" came from the blue-checked veil.

A stir in the shed-room—a half-suppressed cough and a clearing of the throat.

"An' then Dad fell on Pete Petrie at the Crossroads' store, whar the critter hed stopped with his mail-pouch, an' Dad trounced him well afore all the crowd o' loafers thar!"

"Bless the Lord, he did!" the checked apron voiced a melancholy triumph.

"An' then, ye remember whenst Dad set out fire in the woods las' fall ter burn off the trash on his own lan', the flames run jes' a leetle over his line an' on ter them woods on

WHO CROSSES STORM MOUNTAIN?

Storm Mounting, doin' no harm ter nobody, nor nuthin'!"

"Not a mite—not a mite," asseverated the apron.

"An' ez sech appears ter be agin the law Petrie gin information an' Dad war fined five dollars!"

"An' paid it!" cried Jane Gilhooley. "Ye know that!"

"An' then, ez it 'pears ter be the law ez one hundred dollars fur sech an offense is ter be forfeited ter ennybody ez will sue fur it," Medora resumed, "Petrie seen his chance ter git even fur bein' beat in a reg'lar knock-down-an'-drag-out fight, an'," with the rising inflection of a climax, "he hev sued and got jedgmint!"

"An' so what that half-drunk dep'ty, Clem Tweed, calls an execution war leveled!" exclaimed Jane Gilhooley, her veiled head swaying forlornly as she sobbed invisibly.

"But Dad 'lowed ez Peter Petrie shouldn't hev none o' his gear," Medora's eyes flashed with a responsive sentiment.

"His gran'mam's warpin' bars!" suggested the elder woman.

"The spinnin'-wheels she brung from

No'th Carliny," enumerated Medora, "the loom an' the candle-moulds."

"The cheers his dad made fur his mam whenst they begun housekeepin'," said Jane Gilhooley's muffled voice.

"The press an' the safe," Medora continued.

"The pot an' the oven," chokingly responded the apron.

"The churn an' the piggins!"

"The skillet an' the trivet!"

Medora, fairly flinching from the inventory of all the household goods, so desecrated and "leveled on," returned to the salient incident of the day. "Dad jes' tuk an axe an' bust up every yearthly thing in the house!"

"An' now we-uns ain't got nuthin'." The elder woman looked about in stunned dismay, her little black eyes a mere gleam of a pupil in the midst of their swollen lids and network of wrinkles.

One of the miseries of the very ignorant is, paradoxically, the partial character of their privation. If the unknown were to them practically non-existent they might find solace in sluggish and secure content. But even the smallest circle of being touches continually the periphery of wider spheres. The air is freighted with echoes of undistinguished sounds. Powers, illimitable, absolute, uncomprehended, seem to hold an inimical sway over their lives and of these the most dreaded is the benign law, framed for their protection, spreading above them an unperceived, unimagined ægis. Thus there was hardly an article in the house which was not exempt by statute from execution, and the house itself and land worth only a hundred or two dollars were protected by the homestead law. The facetious deputy, Clem Tweed, with "Christmas in his bones," would have committed a misdemeanor in seriously levying upon them. He had held the affair as a capital farce — even affecting with wild, appropriating gambols to seize the baby and the cat—and fully realized that malice only had prompted the whole proceeding, to humiliate Ross Gilhooley and illustrate the completeness of the victory which Peter Petrie had won over his enemy.

The younger Gilhooley, however, quaked as his limited intelligence laid hold on the fact that if the law had permitted a levy on the household goods to satisfy the judgment of Peter Petrie their destruction was in itself a balking of the process, resistance to the law, and with an unimagined penalty.

"We-uns hev got ter git away from hyar somehows!" he said with decision.

The idea of bluff Ross Gilhooley in the clutches of the law because of one fierce moment of goaded and petulant despair, with the ignominy of a criminal accusation, with all the sordid concomitants of arrest and the jail, was infinitely terrible to his unaccustomed imagination. He revolted from its contemplation with a personal application. For an honest man, however poor, feels all the high prerogatives of honor.

There was a step in the shed-room where Ross Gilhooley had lurked and listened. His wrath now spent, his mind had traveled the obvious course to his son's conclusion. He stood a gigantic, bearded shadow in the doorway, half ashamed, wholly repentant, dimly, vaguely fearful, and all responsive and quivering to the idea of flight. "I been studyin' some 'bout goin' ter Minervy Sue's in Georgy," he said creakingly, as if his voice had suffered from its unwonted disuse.

WHO CROSSES STORM MOUNTAIN?

"An' none too soon," said Bruce doggedly. "The oxen is Medory's, bein' lef' ter her whenst her dad died, an' the wagin is mine! Quit foolin' along o' that thar fire, Medory!" For with her bright hair hanging curling over her cheeks his young wife had leaned forward to start it anew.

"Never ter kindle it agin on this ha'thstone!" she cried with a poignant realization of the significance of the uprooting of the roof-tree and the wide, vague world without. And still once more the two women fell to bemoaning their fate of exile beside the expiring embers, while the elder Gilhooley's voice sounded bluffly outside calling the oxen, and his son was rattling their heavy yoke in the corner.

They were well advanced on their journey ere yet the snowy Christmas dawn was in the sky. So slow a progress was ill-associated with the idea of flight. It was almost noiseless—the great hoofs of the oxen fell all muffled on the deep snow still whitely a-glitter with the moon, hanging dense and opaque in the western sky, and flecked with the dendroidal images of the overshadowing trees. The immense bovine heads swayed to and fro, cadenced to the deliberate pace, and more than once a muttered low of distaste and protest rose with the vapor curling upward from lip and nostril into the icy air. On the front seat of the cumbrous, white, canvas-covered vehicle was Medora, her bright hair blowing out from the folds of a red shawl worn hoodwise; she held a cord attached to the horns of one of the oxen by which she sought to guide the yoke in those intervals when her husband, who walked by their side with a goad, must needs fall to the rear to drive up a cow and calf. Inside the wagon Ross Gilhooley did naught but bow his head between his hands as if he could not face the coming day charged with he knew not what destiny for him. His wife was adjusting and readjusting the limited gear they had dared to bring off with them—their forlorn rags of clothing and bedding, all in shapeless bundles; sundry gourds full of soft soap, salt, tobacco, and a scanty store of provisions, which she feared would not last them all the way to Georgia to the home of Minervy Sue, their daughter.

No one touched a space deeply filled with straw, but now and again Medora glanced

WHO CROSSES STORM MOUNTAIN?

back at it with the dawning of a smile in her grief-stricken face that cold, nor fear, nor despair could wholly overcast. Three small heads, all golden and curly, all pink-cheeked and fair, all blissfully slumbering, rested there as if they had been so many dolls packed away thus for fear of breaking. But they had no other couch than the straw, for Ross Gilhooley had not spared the featherbeds, and the little cabin at the Notch was now half full of the fluff ripped out by his sharp knife from the split ticks.

Down the mountain the fugitives went, as silent as their shadows; and at last, when one might hardly know if it were the sheen of the moon that still illuminated the wan and wintry scene, or the reflection from the snow, or the dawning of the dark-gray day, the river came in sight, all a rippling, steely expanse under the chill wind between its ice-girt crags and snowy banks.

The oxen went down to the ford in a lumbering run. Bruce sprang upon the tail-board to ride, the dogs chased the cow and calf to the crossing. The wheels grated ominously against great submerged boulders; the surging waves rose almost to the wagon-

WHO CROSSES STORM MOUNTAIN?

bed; the wind struck aslant the immense, cumbrous cover, threatening to capsize it; and, suddenly, in the midst of the transit, a sound, as clear as a bugle in the rare icy air, as searchingly sweet!

All were motionless for an instant, doubtful, anxious, listening—only the wintry wind with its keen sibilance; only the dash of the swift current; only the grating of the wheels on the sand as the oxen reached the opposite margin!

But hark, again! A clear tenor voice in the fag end of an old song:

" An' my bigges' bottle war my bes' friend,
An' my week's work was all at an end! "

It issued from beyond the right fork of the road in advance, and an instant panic ensued. Discovery was hard upon them. Their laborious device was brought to naught should any eye espy them in their hasty flight to the State line. It had not seemed impossible that ere the day should dawn they might be far away in those impenetrable forests where one may journey many a league, meeting naught more inimical or

WHO CROSSES STORM MOUNTAIN?

speculative than bear or deer. It still was worth the effort.

With a sudden spring from the tailboard of the wagon Bruce Gilhooley reached the yoke, fiercely goading the oxen onward. With an abrupt lurch, in which the vehicle swayed precariously and ponderously from side to side, they started up the steep, snowy bank, and breaking into their ungainly run were guided into the left fork of the road. It was a level stretch and fringed about with pines, and soon all sight of the pilgrims was lost amidst the heavy snow-laden boughs.

The river bank was silent and solitary; and after a considerable interval a man rode down from the right fork to the ford.

More than once his horse refused the passage. A sort of parrot-faced man he was, known as Tank Dysart, young, red-haired, with a long, bent nose and a preposterous air of knowingness and turbulent inquiry. He cocked his head on one side with a snort of surprised indignation, and beat with both heels, but again the horse, sidling about the drifts, declined the direct passage and essayed to cross elsewhere.

All at once a bundle of red flannel, lying

in the drift close to the water's edge, caught his attention, and suddenly there issued forth a lusty bawl. The horseman would have turned pale but for the whisky which had permanently incarnadined the bend of his nose. As it was, however, he looked far more dismayed than the facts might seem to warrant.

" It's the booze—I got 'em again fur sartain! " he quavered in plaintive helplessness, his terrified eyes fixed on the squirming bundle.

Then, drunk as he was, he perceived the rift in his logic. " Gol-darn ye! " he exclaimed, violently kicking the horse, " you-uns ain't got no call ter view visions an' see sights—ye old water-bibber! "

As the horse continued to snort and back away from the object Tank Dysart became convinced of its reality. Still mounted, he passed close enough alongside for a grasp at it. The old red-flannel cape and hood disclosed a plump infant about ten months of age, whimpering and cruelly rubbing his eyes with his fists, and now bawling outright with rage; as he chanced to meet the gaze of his rescuer he paused to laugh in a one-sided way, displaying two pearly teeth and a very beguiling red tongue, but again stiffening himself he yelled as behooves a self-respecting baby so obviously misplaced.

Tank Dysart held him out at arm's length in his strong grasp, surveying him in mingled astonishment and delight. "Why, bless my soul, Christmas gift!" he addressed him. "I'm powerful obligated fur yer company!"

For the genial infant giggled and sputtered and gurgled inconsistently in the midst of his bawling, and banteringly kicked out one soft foot in a snug, red sock, taking Tank full in the chest; then he stiffened, swayed backward and screamed again as if in agonies of grief.

"Sufferin' Moses!" grinned the drunkard. "I wouldn't take nuthin' fur ye! Ye air a find, an' no mistake!" The word suggested illusion. "Ye ain't no snake, now— nary toad—nary green rabbit—no sort'n jim-jam?" he stipulated apprehensively.

The baby babbled gleefully, and, as if attesting its reality, delivered half a dozen strong kicks with those active plump feet, encased in the smart red socks.

It suddenly occurred to the drunkard that here was a duty owing—to seek out the child's parents. Even to his befuddled brain that fact was plain enough. The little creature

WHO CROSSES STORM MOUNTAIN?

had been lost evidently from some family of travelers who would presently retrace their way seeking him.

When Bruce Gilhooley had sprung from the tailboard of the wagon in that moment of tumultuous panic he had not noticed the bundle of straw dislodged. Falling with it softly into the deep snowdrift the child had continued to slumber quietly till awakened by the cold to silence and loneliness, and then this strange rencontre.

With a half-discriminated idea of overtaking the supposed travelers, Tank Dysart briskly forded the river, and, pressing his horse to a canter, made off in the opposite direction.

Gayly they fared along for a time, Tank frequently refreshing himself from a "tickler," facetiously so-called, which he carried in his pocket. Occasionally he generously offered the baby the stopper to suck, and as the child smacked his lips with evident relish Tank roared out again in his fine and flexible tenor:

"For my bigges' bottle war my bes' friend,
An' my week's work war all at an end!"

WHO CROSSES STORM MOUNTAIN?

The horse, by far the nobler animal of the two, stood still ever and anon when the drunken creature swayed back and forth in his saddle, imperiling his equilibrium. Even to his besotted mind, as he grew more intoxicated, the danger to the child in his erratic grasp became apparent.

"I got ter put him in a safe place—a Christmas gift," he now and then stuttered.

When he came at last within reach of a human habitation he had been for some time consciously on the point of falling from the saddle with the infant, who was now quietly asleep. He noted, as in a dream, the Crossroads' store, which was also the post-office; standing in front of the log cabin was a horse already saddled hanging down a dull, dispirited head as he awaited the mail-rider through a long, cold interval, and bearing a United States mail-pouch, mouldy, flabby, nearly empty. The door of the store was closed against the cold; the blacksmith's shop was far down the road; the two or three scattered dwellings showed no sign of life but the wreaths of blue smoke curling up from the clay-and-stick chimneys.

Perhaps it was the impunity of the moment that suggested the idea to Dysart's whimsical drunken fancy. He never knew. He suddenly tried the mouth of the pouch. It was locked. Nothing daunted, a stroke of a keen knife slit the upper part of the side seam, the sleeping baby was slipped into the aperture, and Tank Dysart rode off chuckling with glee to think of the dismay of the mail-rider when the mail-pouch should break forth with squeals and quiver with kicks, which embarrassment would probably not befall him until far away in the wilderness with his perplexity, for there had been something stronger on that stopper than milk or cambric tea.

As Tank went he muttered something about the security of the United States mail, wherein he had had the forethought to deposit his Christmas gift, and forthwith he flung himself into the shuck-pen, where he fell asleep, and was not found till half-frozen, his whereabouts being at last disclosed to the storekeeper by the persistent presence of his faithful steed standing hard by. Tank was humanely cared for by this functionary, but several days elapsed before he altogether recovered consciousness; it was naturally a confused, disconnected train of impressions which his mind retained. At first, in a maudlin state, he demanded of the storekeeper, in his capacity as postmaster also, a package, a Christmas gift, which he averred he should receive by mail. Albeit this was esteemed merely an inebriated fancy, such is the sensitiveness of the United States postal service on the subject of missing mail matter that the postmaster, half-irritated, half-nervous, detailed it to the mail-rider. "Tank 'lows ez he put it into the mail hyar himself!"

Peter Petrie, a lowering-eyed, severe-visaged, square-jawed man, gave Tank Dysart only a glance of ire from under his hat-brim, as if the matter were not worth the waste of a word.

Dysart, wreck though he was, had not yet lost all conscience. He was in an agony of remorse and doubt. It kept him sober longer than he had been for five years, for he was a professed drunkard and idler, scarcely considered responsible. He could not be sure that he had experienced aught which he seemed to remember—he hoped it was all only his drunken fancy, for what could have been

WHO CROSSES STORM MOUNTAIN?

the fate of the child subject to the freaks of his imbecile folly? He was reassured to hear no rumors of a lost child, and yet so definite were the images of his recollection that they must needs constrain his credulity.

He felt it in the nature of a rescue one day when, as he chanced to join a group of gossips loitering around the fire of the forge, he heard the smith ask casually: " Who is that thar baby visitin' at Peter Petrie's over yander acrost Storm Mounting?"

" Gran'child, I reckon," suggested his big-boned, bare-armed, soot-grimed striker.

" Peter Petrie hain't got nare gran'- child," said one of the loungers.

Tank, sober for once, held his breath to listen.

"Behaves powerful like a gran'dad," observed the smith, holding a horseshoe with the tongs in the fire while the striker laid hold on the bellows and the sighing sound surged to and fro and the white blaze flared forth, showing the interested faces of the group in the dusky smithy, and among them the horse whose shoe was making, while another stood at the open door defined against the snow. " Behaves like he ain't got a mite o' sense. I

WHO CROSSES STORM MOUNTAIN?

war goin' by thar one day las' week an' I stepped up on the porch ter pass the time o' day with Pete an' his wife, an' the door war open. And' what d'ye s'pose I seen? Old Peter Petrie a-goin' round the floor on all fours, an' a-settin' on his back war a baby—powerful peart youngster—jes' a-grinnin' an' a-whoopin' an' a-poundin' old Peter with a whip! An' Pete galloped, he did! Didn't seem beset with them rheumatics he used ter talk about—peartest leetle 'possum of a baby!"

Tank Dysart lost no time in his investigations and he had the courage of his convictions. He did not scruple to call Peter Petrie to his face a mail-robber.

"Ye tuk a package deposited in the United States' mail and converted it to your own use," he vociferated.

" 'Twar neither stamped nor addressed," old Petrie gruffly contended, albeit obviously disconcerted.

Dysart even sought to induce the postmaster to send a complaint of the rider to the postal authorities.

" I got too much respec' fur my job," replied that worthy, jocosely eying Tank across

WHO CROSSES STORM MOUNTAIN?

the counter of the store. "I ain't goin' ter let on ter the folks in Washington that we send babies about in the mail-bags hyar in the mountings."

The social acquaintance of the little man had necessarily been rather limited, but one day a neighbor, attracted to the Petrie cabin by idle curiosity concerning the waif robbed from the mails, gazed upon him for one astonished instant and then proclaimed his identity.

"Nare Gilhooley should ever cross Storm Mounting, 'cordin ter yer sayin', Petey, an' hyar ye hev been totin' Ross Gilhooley's gran'son back an' forth across Old Stormy, an' all yer spare time ye spend on yer hands an' knees barkin' like a dog jes' ter pleasure him."

Peter Petrie changed countenance suddenly. His square, bristly, grim jaw hardened and stiffened, so dear to him were all his stubborn convictions and grizzly, ancient feuds. But he bestirred himself to cause information to be conveyed to Bruce Gilhooley of his son's whereabouts for he readily suspected that the family had fled to Minervy Sue's in Georgia. Peter Petrie sustained in this act of conscience a grievous wrench, for it foreshadowed parting with the choice missive filched from the mail-bag, but he was not unmindful of the anguish and bereavement of the mother, and somehow the thought was peculiarly coercive at this season.

"I don't want ter even up with King Herod, now, sure!" he averred to himself one night as he sat late over the embers, reviewing his plans all made. He thought much in these lone hours as he heard the wind speed past, the trees crack under their weight of snow, and noted through the tiny window the glister of a great star of a supernal lustre, high above the pines, what a freight of joy the tidings of this child would bear to the bleeding hearts of his kindred. Albeit so humble, the parallel must needs arise suggesting the everlasting joy the existence of another Child had brought to the souls of all kindreds, all peoples. "Peace, peace," he reiterated, as the red coals crumbled and the gray ash spread; "Peace an' good-will!"

The words seemed to epitomize all religion, all value, all hope, and somehow they so dwelt in his mind that the next day he was moved to add a personal message to old Ross Gilhooley in sending the more important information to Bruce.

"Let on ter Ross," he charged the envoy, "ez—ez—that thar jedgmint an' execution issued war jes' formal—ye mought say—jes' ter hev all the papers reg'lar."

By virtue of more attrition with the world the mail-rider was more sophisticated than his enemy, and sooth to say, more sophistical.

"Ross is writ-proof, the old fool, though he war minded ter cut me out'n my levy if he could! But waal, jes' tell him from me ez we-uns hev hed a heap o' pleasure in the baby's company in the Chris'mus, an' we-uns expec' ter borry him some whenst they all gits home!"

To the child's kindred the news was as if he had risen from the dead, and the gratitude of the Gilhooleys to Petrie knew no bounds. They had accounted the baby drowned when, missing him, they had retraced their way, finding naught but a bit of old blanket on which he had lain, close to the verge of the cruel river. Ross Gilhooley, softened and rendered tractable by exile and sorrow, upon

WHO CROSSES STORM MOUNTAIN?

his return lent himself to an affected warmth toward Peter Petrie which gradually assumed all the fervors of sincerity. The neighbors indeed were moved to say that the two friends and ancient enemies, when both on all fours and barking for the delight of the baby, were never so little like dogs in all their lives.

Thus a child shall lead them.

THE CRUCIAL MOMENT

A mere moment seems an inconsiderable factor in life—only its multiplication attaining importance and signifying time. It could never have occurred to Walter Hoxer that all his years of labor, the aggregation of the material values of industry, experience, skill, integrity, could be nullified by this minimum unit of space—as sudden, as potent, as destructive, as a stroke of lightning. But after the fact it did not remind him of any agency of the angry skies; to him it was like one of the obstructions of the river engineers to divert the course of the great Mississippi, a mattress-spur, a thing insignificant in itself, a mere trifle of woven willow wands, set up at a crafty angle, against the tumultuous current. Yet he had seen the swirling waves, in their oncoming like innumerable herds of wild horses, hesitate at the impact, turn aside, and go racing by, scouring out a new channel, leaving the old bank bereft, thrown inland, no longer the margin of the stream.

The river was much in his mind that after-

THE CRUCIAL MOMENT

noon as he trudged along the county road at the base of the levee, on his way, all unprescient, to meet this signal, potential moment. Outside, he knew that the water was standing higher than his head, rippling against the thick turf of Bermuda grass with which the great earthwork was covered. For the river was bank-full and still rising—indeed, it was feared that an overflow impended. However, there was as yet no break; advices from up the river and down the river told only of extra precautions and constant work to keep the barriers intact against the increasing volume of the stream. The favorable chances were reinforced by the fact of a singularly dry winter, that had so far eliminated the danger from back-water, which, if aggregated from rainfall in low-lying swamps, would move up slowly to inundate the arable lands. These were already ploughed to bed up for cotton, and an overflow now would mean the loss of many thousands of dollars to the submerged communities. The February rains had begun in the upper country, with a persistency and volume that bade fair to compensate for the long-continued drought, and thus the river was already booming; the bayous that drew off a vast surplusage of its waters were overcharged, and gradually would spread out in murky shallows, heavily laden with river detritus, over the low grounds bordering their course.

"This Jeffrey levee will hold," Hoxer said to himself, as once he paused, his hands in his pockets, his cap on the back of his red head, his freckled, commonplace, square face lifted into a sort of dignity by the light of expert capacity and intelligence in his bluff blue eyes. He had been muttering to himself the details of its construction: so many feet across the base in proportion to its height, the width of the summit, the angle of the incline of its interior slope—the exterior being invisible, having the Mississippi River standing against it. "A fairly good levee, though an old one," he muttered. "I'll bet, though, Major Jeffrey feels mightily like Noah when he looks at all that water out there tearing through the country."

His face clouded at the mention of the name, and as he took the short pipe from his mouth and stuck it into the pocket of his loose sack-coat his tread lost a certain free elasticity that had characterized it hitherto, and he trudged on doggedly. He had passed many acres of ploughed lands, the road running between the fields and the levee. The scene was all solitary; the sun had set, and night would presently be coming on. As he turned in at the big white gate that opened on a long avenue of oaks leading to the mansion house, he began to fear that his visit might be ill-timed, and that a man of his station could not hope for an audience so near the major's dinner-hour.

It was with definite relief that he heard the gentle impact of ivory balls in the absolute quiet, and he remembered that a certain little octagonal structure with a conical red roof, in the grounds, was a billiard-room, for the sound betokened that he might find the owner of the place here.

He expected to see a group of the Major's "quality friends" in the building but as he ascended the steps leading directly to the door, he perceived that the man he sought was alone. Major Jeffrey was engaged in idly knocking the balls about in some skilful fancy shots, his cigar in his mouth, and a black velvet smoking-jacket setting off to special advantage his dense, snowy hair, prematurely white, his long mustache, and his pointed imperial. His heavy white eyebrows drew frowningly together over arrogant dark eyes as he noted the man at the entrance.

Despite Hoxer's oft-reiterated sentiment that he was "as good as anybody and would take nothing off nobody, and cared for no old duck just because he was rich," he could not speak for a moment as he felt Major Jeffrey's inimical eyes upon him. He lost the advantage in losing the salutation.

"Did you get my check?" Major Jeffrey asked curtly.

"Yes," Hoxer admitted; "but——"

"The amount was according to contract."

Hoxer felt indignant with himself that he should have allowed this interpretation to be placed on his presence here; then he still more resented the conjecture.

"I have not come for extra money," he said. "That point of the transaction is closed."

"All the points of the transaction are

THE CRUCIAL MOMENT

closed," said Major Jeffrey, ungraciously. There was more than the flush of the waning western sky on his face. He had already dined, and he was one of those wine-bibbers whom drink does not render genial. " I want to hear no more about it."

He turned to the table, and with a skilful cue sent one ball caroming against two others.

" But you must hear what I have got to say, Major Jeffrey," protested Hoxer. " I built that cross-levee for you to join your main levee, and done it well."

" And have been well paid."

" But you go and say at the store that I deviated from the line of survey and saved one furlong, seven poles, and five feet of levee."

" And so you did."

" But you know, Major, that Burbeck Lake had shrunk in the drought at the time of the survey, and if I'd followed the calls for the south of the lake, I'd had to build in four feet of water, so I drew back a mite—you bein' in Orleans, where I couldn't consult you, an' no time to be lost nohow, the river bein' then on the rise, an'——"

THE CRUCIAL MOMENT

"Look here, fellow," exclaimed Major Jeffrey, bringing the cue down on the table with a force that must have cut the cloth, "do you suppose that I have nothing better to do than to stand here to listen to your fool harangue?"

The anger and the drink and perhaps the consciousness of being in the wrong were all ablaze in the Major's eyes.

The two were alone; only the darkling shadows stood at tiptoe at the open windows, and still the flushed sky sent down a pervasive glow from above.

Hoxer swallowed hard, gulping down his own wrath and sense of injury. "Major," he said blandly, trying a new deal, "I don't think you quite understand me."

"Such a complicated proposition you are, to be sure!"

Hoxer disregarded the sarcasm, the contempt in the tone.

"I am not trying to rip up an old score, but you said at Winfield's store—at the store —that I did not build the cross levee on the surveyor's line; that I shortened it——"

"So you did."

"But as if I had shortened the levee for

THE CRUCIAL MOMENT

my own profit, when, as you know, it was paid for by the pole——"

"You tax me with making a false impression?"

An extreme revulsion of expectation harassed Hoxer. He had always known that Jeffrey was an exception to the general rule of the few large land-owners in the community, who were wont to conserve and, in fact, to deserve the pose of kindly patron as well as wealthy magnate. But even Jeffrey, he thought, would not grudge a word to set a matter straight that could cost him nothing and would mean much to the levee-contractor. Though of large experience in levee-building, Hoxer was new to the position of contractor, having been graduated into it, so to speak, from the station of foreman of a construction-gang of Irishmen. He had hoped for further employ in this neighborhood, in building private levees that, in addition to the main levees along the banks of the Mississippi, would aid riparian protection by turning off overflow from surcharged bayous and encroaching lakes in the interior. But, unluckily, the employer of the first enterprise he had essayed on his own responsibility had declared that he had deviated from the line of survey, usually essential to the validity of the construction, thereby much shortening the work; and had made this statement at Winfield's store—at the store!

Whatever was said at the store was as if proclaimed through the resounding trump of fame. The store in a Mississippi neighborhood, frequented by the surrounding planters, great and small, was the focus of civilization, the dispenser of all the wares of the world, from a spool of thread to a two-horse wagon, the post-office, in a manner the club. Here, sooner or later, everybody came, and hence was the news of the Bend noised abroad. Hoxer's business could scarcely recover from this disparagement, and he had not doubted that Jeffrey would declare that he had said nothing to justify this impression, and that he would forthwith take occasion to clear it up. For were not Mr. Tompkins and Judge Claris, both with a severe case of "high-water scare," ready to contract for a joint cross levee for mutual protection from an unruly bayou!

Therefore, with a sedulous effort, Hoxer maintained his composure when the Major thundered again, " You tax me with making a false impression? "

" Not intentionally, Major, but——"

" And who are you to judge of my motives? Told a lie by accident, did I? Begone, sir, or I'll break your head with this billiard cue! "

He had reached the limit as he brandished the cue. He was still agile, vigorous, and it was scarcely possible that Hoxer could escape the blow. He dreaded the indignity indeed more than the hurt.

" If you strike me," he declared in a single breath, between his set teeth, " before God, I'll shoot you with your own pistol! "

It seemed a fatality that a pair in their open case should have been lying on the sill of the window, where their owner had just been cleaning and oiling them. Hoxer, of course, had no certainty that they were loaded, but the change in Jeffrey's expression proclaimed it. He was sober enough now—the shock was all sufficient—as he sprang to the case. The younger man was the quicker. He had one of the pistols in his hand before Jeffrey could level the other that he had snatched. Quicker to fire, too, for the weapon in Jeffrey's hand was discharged in his latest impulse of action after he fell to the floor, the blood gushing from a wound that crimsoned all the delicate whiteness of his shirt-front and bedabbled his snowy hair and beard.

This was the moment, the signal, fatal, final moment, that the levee contractor had come to meet, that placed the period to his own existence. He lived no longer, Hoxer felt. He did not recognize as his own a single action hereafter, a single mental impulse. It was something else, standing here in the red gloaming—some foreign entity, cogently reasoning, swiftly acting. Self-defense—was it? And who would believe that? Had he found justice so alert to redress his wrongs, even in a little matter, that he must needs risk his neck upon it? This Thing that was not himself—no, never more!—had the theory of alibi in his mind as he stripped off his low-cut shoes and socks, thrusting them into his pockets, leaping from the door, and flying among the dusky shadows down the gloaming grove, and through the gate.

Dusk here, too, on the lonely county road,

THE CRUCIAL MOMENT

the vague open expanse of the ploughed fields glimmering to the instarred sky of a still, chill night of early February. He did not even wonder that there should be no hue and cry on his tracks—the Thing was logical! Jeffrey had doubtless had his pistols carried down from the mansion to him in his den in the billiard-room, for the avowed purpose of putting the weapons in order. If the shots were heard at all at the dwelling, the sound was reasonably ascribed to the supposed testing of the weapons. Hoxer was conscious that a sentiment of gratulation, of sly triumph, pervaded his mental processes as he sped along barefoot, like some tramp or outcast, or other creature of a low station. He had laid his plans well in this curious, involuntary cerebration. Those big, bare footprints were ample disguise for a well-clad, well-groomed, well-shod middle-class man of a skilful and lucrative employ. The next moment his heart sank like lead. He was followed! He heard the pursuit in the dark! Swift, unerring, leaping along the dusty road, leaving its own footprints as a testimony against him. For he had recognized its

THE CRUCIAL MOMENT

nature at last! It was his own dog—a little, worthless cur, that had a hide like a doormat and a heart as big as the United States —a waif, a stray, that had attached himself to the contractor at the shanties of the construction gang, and slept by his bed, and followed at his heel, and lived on the glance of his eye.

He was off again, the dog fairly winging his way to match his master's speed. Hoxer could not kill him here, for the carcass would tell the story. But was it not told already in those tracks in the dusty road? What vengeance was there not written in the eccentric script of those queer little padded imprints of the creature's paws. Fie, fool! Was this the only cur-dog in the Bend? he asked himself, impatient of his fears. Was not the whole neighborhood swarming with canine dependents?

Despite his reasoning, this endowment that was once himself had been affrighted by the shock. The presence of the little curdog had destroyed the complacence of his boasted ratiocination. He had only the instincts of flight as he struck off through the woods when the great expanse of culti-

THE CRUCIAL MOMENT

vated lands had given way to lower ground and the wide liberties of the " open swamp," as it was called. This dense wilderness stretched out on every side; the gigantic growth of gum trees was leafless at this season, and without a suggestion of underbrush. The ground was as level as a floor. Generally during the winter the open swamp is covered with shallow water, but in this singularly droughty season it had remained " with dry feet," according to the phrase of that country. The southern moon, rising far along its levels, began to cast burnished golden shafts of light adown its unobstructed vistas. It might seem some magnificent park, with its innumerable splendid trees, its great expanse, and ever and anon in the distance the silver sheen of the waters of a lake, shining responsive to the lunar lustre as with an inherent lustre of its own.

On and on he went, his noiseless tread falling as regularly as machinery, leaving miles behind him, the distance only to be conjectured by the lapse of time, and, after so long, his flagging strength. He began to notice that the open swamp was giving way in the vicinity of one of the lakes to the characteristics of the swamp proper, although the ground was still dry and the going good. He had traversed now and then a higher ridge on which switch-cane grew somewhat sparsely, but near the lake on a bluff bank a dense brake of the heavier cane filled the umbrageous shadows, so tall and rank and impenetrable a growth that once the fugitive paused to contemplate it with the theory that a secret intrusted to its sombre seclusions might be held intact forever.

As he stood thus motionless in the absolute stillness, a sudden thought came to his mind—a sudden and terrible thought. He could not be sure whether he had heard aught, or whether the sight of the water suggested the idea. He knew that he could little longer sustain his flight, despite his vigor and strength. Quivering in every fibre from his long exertions, he set his course straight for that glimmering sheen of water. Encircling it were heavy shadows. Tall trees pressed close to the verge, where lay here a fallen branch, and there a rotten log, half sunken in mud and ooze, and again a great tangle of vines that had grown

THE CRUCIAL MOMENT

smiling to the summer sun, but now, with the slow expansion of the lake which was fed by a surcharged bayou, quite submerged in a fretwork of miry strands. The margin was fringed with saw-grass, thick and prickly, and his practised eye could discern where the original banks lay by the spears thrust up above the surface a score of feet away. Thus he was sure of his depth as he waded out staunchly, despite the cruel pricks to his sensitive naked feet. The little dog had scant philosophy; he squeaked and wheezed and wailed with the pain until the man, who had no time to kill him now—for had he heard aught or naught?—picked him up and carried him in his arms, the creature licking Hoxer's hands in an ecstasy of gratitude, and even standing on his hind-legs on his master's arm to snatch a lick upon his cheek.

In the darksome shadows, further and further from the spot where he had entered the lake, Hoxer toiled along the margin, sometimes pausing to listen—for had he heard aught or naught?—as long as his strength would suffice. Then amidst the miry débris of last summer's growths beneath the recent inundation he sank down in the darkness, the dog exhausted in his arms.

This was one of those frequent crescent-shaped lakes peculiar to the region; sometimes, miles in extent, the lacustrine contour is not discernible to the glance; here the broad expanse seemed as if the body of water were circular and perhaps three miles in diameter.

Suddenly Hoxer heard the sound that had baffled him hitherto—heard it again and —oh, horrible!—recognized it at last! The baying of bloodhounds it was, the triumphant cry that showed that the brutes had caught the trail and were keeping it. On and on came the iteration, ever louder, ever nearer, waking the echoes till wood and brake and midnight waters seemed to rock and sway with the sound, and the stars in the sky to quake in unison with the vibrations. Never at fault, never a moment's cessation, and presently the shouts of men and the tramp of horses blended with that deep, tumultuous note of blood crying to heaven for vengeance. Far, far, down the lake it was. Hoxer could see nothing of the

THE CRUCIAL MOMENT

frantic rout when the hounds paused baffled at the water-side. He was quick to note the changed tone of the brutes' pursuit, plaintive, anxious, consciously thwarted. They ran hither and thither, patrolling the banks, and with all their boasted instinct they could only protest that the fugitive took to water at this spot. But how? They could not say, and the men argued in vain. The lake was too broad to swim—there was no island, no point of vantage. A boat might have taken him off, and, if so, the craft would now be lying on the opposite bank. A party set off to skirt the edge of the lake and explore the further shores by order of the sheriff, for this officer, summoned by telephone, had come swiftly from the county town in an automobile, to the verge of the swamp, there accommodated with a horse by a neighboring planter. And then, Hoxer, lying on the elastic submerged brush, with only a portion of his face above the surface of the water, watched in a speechless ecstasy of terror the hue and cry progress on the hither side, his dog, half dead from exhaustion, unconscious in his arms.

The moon, unmoved as ever, looked

THE CRUCIAL MOMENT

calmly down on the turmoil in the midst of the dense woods. The soft brilliance illumined the long, open vistas and gave to the sylvan intricacies an effect as of silver arabesques, a glittering tracery amidst the shadows. But the lunar light did not suffice. Great torches of pine knots, with a red and yellow flare and streaming pennants of smoke, darted hither and thither as the officer's posse searched the bosky recesses without avail.

Presently a new sound!—a crashing iteration—assailed the air. A frantic crowd was beating the bushes about the margin of the lake and the verges of the almost impenetrable cane-brake. Here, however, there could be no hope of discovery, and suddenly a cry arose, unanimously iterated the next instant, "Fire the cane-brake! Fire the cane-brake!"

For so late had come the rise of the river, so persistent had been the winter's drought, so delayed the usual inundation of the swamp, that the vegetation, dry as tinder, caught the sparks instantly, and the fierce expedient to force the fugitive to leave his supposed shelter in the brake, a vast wood-

THE CRUCIAL MOMENT

land conflagration, was added to the terror of the scene. The flames flared frantically upward from the cane, itself twenty feet in height, and along its dense columns issued forth jets like the volleyings of musketry from serried ranks of troops, the illusion enhanced by continuous sharp, rifle-like reports, the joints of the growth exploding as the air within was liberated by the heat of the fire. All around this blazing Gehenna were swiftly running figures of men applying with demoniac suggestion torches here and there, that a new area might be involved. Others were mounted, carrying flaming torches aloft, the restive horses plunging in frantic terror of the fiery furnace in the depths of the brake, the leaping sheets of flame, the tumultuous clouds of smoke. Oh, a terrible fate, had the forlorn fugitive sought refuge here! Let us hope that no poor denizen of the brake, bear or panther or fox, dazed by the tumult and the terror, forgot which way to flee!

But human energies must needs fail as time wears on. Nerves of steel collapse at last. The relinquishment of the quest came gradually; the crowd thinned; now and again the sound of rapid hoof-beats told of homeward-bound horsemen; languid groups stood and talked dully here and there, dispersing to follow a new suggestion for a space, then ultimately disappearing; even the fire began to die out, and the site of the cane-break had become a dense, charred mass, as far as eye could reach, with here and there a vague blue flicker where some bed of coals could yet send up a jet, when at length the pale day, slow and aghast, came peering along the levels to view the relics of the strange events that had betided in the watches of the night.

Hoxer had not waited for the light. Deriving a certain strength, a certain triumph, from the obvious fact that the end was not yet, he contrived in that darkest hour before the dawn to pull himself into a sitting posture, then to creep out to the shore. The little dog had seemed to be dying, but he too experienced a sort of resuscitation, and while he followed at first but feebly, it was not long before he was at heel again, although Hoxer was swift of foot, making all the speed he might toward his temporary home, the shacks that had been occupied by

THE CRUCIAL MOMENT

the construction gang. As he came within view of the poor little tenements, so recently vacated by the Irish ditchers, all awry and askew, stretching in a wavering row along the river-bank near the junction of the levee that he had built with the main line, his eyes filled. Oh, why had he not gone with the rest of the camp? he demanded of an untoward fate; why must he have stayed a day longer to bespeak the correction of an injurious error from that proud, hard man, who, however, had wrought his last injury on earth? Hoxer was sorry, but chiefly for his own plight. He felt that his deed was in self-defense, and but that he had no proof he would not fear to offer the plea at the bar of justice. As it was, however, he was sanguine of escaping without this jeopardy. No one had cause to suspect him. No one had seen him enter the Jeffrey grounds that fatal evening. There had been noised abroad no intimation of his grievance against the man. He had all the calm assurance of invisibility as he came to his abode, for a fog lay thick on the surface of the river and hung over all the land. He did not issue forth again freshly dressed

THE CRUCIAL MOMENT

till the sun was out once more, dispelling the vapors and conjuring the world back to sight and life. Nevertheless, he made no secret of having been abroad when an acquaintance came up the road and paused for an exchange of the news of the day.

"But what makes ye look so durned peaked?" he broke off, gazing at Hoxer in surprise.

Hoxer was astonished at his own composure as he replied: "Out all night. I was in the swamp with the posse."

"See the fire? They tell me 't wuz more'n dangerous to fire the brake when the woods is so uncommon dry. I dunno what we would do here in the bottom with a forest fire."

"Pretty big blaze now, sure's ye're born," Hoxer replied casually, and so the matter passed.

Later in the day another gossip, whose acquaintance he had made during his levee-building venture, loitered up to talk over the absorbing sensation, and, sitting down on the door-step of the shack, grew suddenly attentive to the little dog.

THE CRUCIAL MOMENT

"What makes him limp?" he demanded abruptly.

But Hoxer had not observed that he did limp.

The acquaintance had taken the little animal up on his knee and was examining into his condition. "Gee! how did he get so footsore?"

"Following me around, I reckon," Hoxer hazarded. But he saw, or thought he saw, a change on the stolid face of the visitor, who was unpleasantly impressed with the fact that the officers investigating the case had made inquiries concerning a small dog that, to judge by the prints in the road, had evidently followed the big, barefooted man who had fled from the Jeffrey precincts after the shooting. A rumor, too, was going the rounds that a detective, reputed preternaturally sharp, who had accompanied the sheriff to the scene of action, had examined these tracks in the road, and declared that the foot-print was neither that of a negro nor a tramp, but of a white man used to wearing shoes something too tightly fitting.

The visitor glanced down at the substantial foot-gear of the contractor, fitting somewhat snugly, and thereafter he became more out of countenance than before and manifested some haste to get away. Hoxer said to himself that his anxiety whetted his apprehension. He had given his visitor no cause for suspicion, and doubtless the man had evolved none. Hoxer was glad that he was due and overdue to be gone from the locality. He felt that he could scarcely breathe freely again till he had joined the gang of Irish ditchers now establishing themselves in a new camp in the adjoining county, where the high stage of the river gave him employment in fighting water. He made up his mind, however, that he would not take the train thither. He dreaded to be among men, to encounter question and speculation, till he had time to regain control of his nerves, his facial expression, the tones of his voice. He resolved that he would quietly drift down the river in a row-boat that had been at his disposal during his employment here, and join his force already settled at their destination, without running the gauntlet of inspection by the neighborhood in a more formal departure. He had

THE CRUCIAL MOMENT

already bidden farewell to those few denizens of the Bend with whom his associations had been most genial. "And I'll clear out now, as I would have done if nothing had happened."

He said no more of his intention of departure, but when night had come he fastened the door of the little shanty, in which were still some of the rude belongings of his camping outfit, with the grim determination that it should not soon be opened again. How long the padlock should beat the summons of the wind on the resounding battens he did not dream!

It was close on midnight when he climbed the steep interior slope of the levee and stood for a moment gazing cautiously about him. The rowboat lay close by, for one might embark from the summit of the levee. It was a cloudy night, without a star. A mist clung to the face of the waters on the Arkansas side, but on the hither shore the atmosphere was clear, for he could see at a considerable distance up the river the fire of a "levee-watch," the stage of the water being so menacing that a guard must needs be on duty throughout the night. The leaping flames of the fire cast long lines of red and yellow and a sort of luminous brown far into the river, where the reflection seemed to palpitate in the pulsations of the current. No other sign of life was in the night scene, save in the opposite direction, amidst the white vapors, the gem-like gleam of a steamer's chimney-lights, all ruby and emerald, as a packet was slowly rounding the neighboring point. Hoxer could hear the impact of her paddles on the water, the night being so still. He had seated himself in the middle of the rowboat and laid hold on the oars when his foot struck against something soft on the bottom of the craft, partly under the seat in the stern. It was his bundle, he thought, containing the spoiled clothing that he had worn in the swamp, and which he intended to sink in mid-stream. His nerve was shaken, however; he could not restrain a sudden exclamation—this must have seemed discovery rather than agitation. It was as a signal for premature action. He was suddenly seized from behind, his arms held down against his sides, his hands close together. The bundle in the stern rose all at once to the stature of a man.

THE CRUCIAL MOMENT

The touch of cold metal, a sharp, quick click, —and he was captured and handcuffed within the space of ten seconds.

A terrible struggle ensued, which his great strength but sufficed to prolong. His wild, hoarse cries of rage and desperation seemed to beat against the sky; back and forth the dark riparian forests repeated them with the effect of varying distance in the echoes, till all the sombre woods seemed full of mad, frantic creatures, shrieking out their helpless frenzy. More than once his superior muscle sufficed to throw off both the officers for a moment, but to what avail? Thus manacled, he could not escape.

Suddenly a wild, new clamor resounded from the shore. In the dusky uncertainty, a group of men were running down the bank, shouting out to the barely descried boatmen imperative warnings that they would break the levee in their commotion, coupled with violent threats if they did not desist. For the force with which the rowboat dashed against the summit of the levee, rebounding again and again, laden with the weight of three ponderous men, and endowed with all the impetus of their struggle, so eroded the earth that the waves had gained an entrance, the initial step to a crevasse that would flood the country with a disastrous overflow. As there was no abatement of the blows of the boat against the embankment, no reply nor explanation, a shot from the gun of one of the levee-watch came skipping lightsomely over the water as Hoxer was borne exhausted to the bottom of the skiff. Then, indeed, the sheriff of the county bethought himself to shout out his name and official station to the astonished group on shore, and thus, bullet-proof under the ægis of the law, the boat pulled out toward the steamer, lying in mid-stream, silently awaiting the coming of the officer and his prisoner, a great, towering, castellated object, half seen in the night, her broadside of cabin lights, and their reflection in the ripples, sparkling through the darkness like a chain of golden stars.

They left no stress of curiosity behind them; naught in the delta can compete in interest with the threatened collapse of a levee in times of high water. Before the rowboat had reached the steamer's side, its occupants could hear the great plantation-bell ringing like mad to summon forth into

THE CRUCIAL MOMENT

the midnight all available hands to save the levee, and, looking back presently, a hundred lanterns were seen flickering hither and thither, far down in the dusk—no illusion this, for all deltaic rivers are higher in the centre than their banks—where the busy laborers, with thousands of gunny-sacks filled with sand, were fighting the Mississippi, building a barricade to fence it from the rich spoils it coveted.

The packet, which, as it happened, was already overdue, had been telephoned by the officers at her last landing, and a number of men stood on the guards expectant. Hoxer had ceased to struggle. He looked up at the steamer, his pallid face and wide, distended eyes showing in the cabin lights, as the rowboat pulled alongside. Then as the sheriff directed him to rise, he stood up at his full height, stretched his manacled hands high above his head, and suddenly dived into deep water, leaving the boat rocking violently, and in danger of capsizing with the officers.

A desperate effort was made to recover the prisoner, alive or dead—all in vain. A roustabout on the deck declared that in the

THE CRUCIAL MOMENT

glare of the steamer's search-light, thrown over the murky waters, he was seen to come to the surface once, but if he rose a second time it must have been beneath the great bulk of the packet, to go down again to the death awaiting him in the deeps.

On the bank a little dog sat through sunshine and shadow in front of the door of the shack of the contractor of the levee-construction gang, and awaited his return with the patient devotion of his kind. Sometimes, as the padlock wavered in the wind, he would cock his head briskly askew, forecasting from the sound a step within. Sometimes the grief of absence and hope deferred would wring his humble heart, and he would whimper in an access of misery and limp about a bit. But presently he would be seated again, alertly upright, his eyes on the door, for the earliest glimpse of the face that he loved. When the overflow came at last the shacks of the construction gang were swept away, and the little dog was seen no more.

UNA OF THE HILL COUNTRY

The old sawmill on Headlong Creek at the water-gap of Chilhowee Mountain was silent and still one day, its habit of industry suggested only in the ample expanse of sawdust spread thickly over a level open space in the woods hard by, to serve as footing for the "bran dance" that had been so long heralded and that was destined to end so strangely.

A barbecue had added its attractions, unrivalled in the estimation of the rustic epicure, but even while the shoats, with the delectable flavor imparted by underground roasting and browned to a turn, were under discussion by the elder men and the sun-bonneted matrons on a shady slope near the mill, where tablecloths had been spread beside a crystal spring, the dance went ceaselessly on, as if the flying figures were insensible of fatigue, impervious to hunger, immune from heat.

Indeed the youths and maidens of the contiguous coves and ridges had rarely so eligible an opportunity, for it is one of the accepted tenets of the rural religionist that dancing in itself is a deadly sin, and all the pulpits of the countryside had joined in fulminations against it. Nothing less than a political necessity had compassed this joyous occasion. It was said to have been devised by the " machine " to draw together the largest possible crowd, that certain candidates might present their views on burning questions of more than local importance, in order to secure vigorous and concerted action at the polls in the luke-warm rural districts when these measures should go before the people, in the person of their advocates, at the approaching primary elections. However, even the wisdom of a political boss is not infallible, and despite the succulent graces of the barbecue numbers of the ascetic and jeans-clad elder worthies, though fed to repletion, collogued unhappily together among the ox-teams and canvas-hooded wagons on the slope, commenting sourly on the frivolity of the dance. These might be relied on to cast no ballots in the interest of its promoters, with whose views they were to be favored between the close of the feast and the final dance before sunset.

UNA OF THE HILL COUNTRY

The trees waved full-foliaged branches above the circle of sawdust and dappled the sunny expanse with flickering shade, and as they swayed apart in the wind they gave evanescent glimpses of tiers on tiers of the faint blue mountains of the Great Smoky Range in the distance, seeming ethereal, luminous, seen from between the dark, steep, wooded slopes of the narrow watergap hard by, through which Headlong Creek plunged and roared. The principal musician, perched with his fellows on a hastily erected stand, was burly, red-faced, and of a jovial aspect. He had a brace of fiddlers, one on each side, but with his own violin under his double-chin he alone " called the figures " of the old-fashioned contradances. Now and again, with a wide, melodious, sonorous voice, he burst into a snatch of song:

"Shanghai chicken he grew so tall,
　In a few days—few days,
　Cannot hear him crow at all——"

Sometimes he would intersperse jocund personal remarks in his Terpsichorean commands: " Gents, forward to the centre—

back—swing the lady ye love the best." Then in alternation, "Ladies, forward to the centre—back——" and as the mountain damsels teetered in expectation of the usual supplement of this mandate he called out in apparent expostulation, "*Don't* swing him, Miss—he don't wuth a turn."

Suddenly the tune changed and with great gusto he chanted forth:

" When fust I did a-courtin' go,
Says she ' Now, *don't* be foolish, Joe,' "

the *tempo rubato* giving fresh impetus to the kaleidoscopic whirl of the dancers. The young men were of indomitable endurance and manifested a crude agility as they sprang about clumsily in time to the scraping of the fiddles, while their partners shuffled bouncingly or sidled mincingly according to their individual persuasion of the most apt expression of elegance. Considered from a critical point of view the dance was singularly devoid of grace—only one couple illustrating the exception to the rule. The youth it was who was obviously beautiful, of a type as old as the fabled Endymion.

UNA OF THE HILL COUNTRY

His long brown hair hung in heavy curls to the collar of his butternut jeans coat; his eyes were blue and large and finely set; his face was fair and bespoke none of the midday toil at the plow-handles that had tanned the complexion of his compeers, for Brent Kayle had little affinity for labor of any sort. He danced with a light firm step, every muscle supplely responsive to the strongly marked pulse of the music, and he had a lithe, erect carriage which imparted a certain picturesque effect to his presence, despite his much creased boots, drawn over his trousers to the knee, and his big black hat which he wore on the back of his head. The face of his partner had a more subtle appeal, and so light and willowy was her figure as she danced that it suggested a degree of slenderness that bordered on attenuation. Her unbonneted hair of a rich blonde hue had a golden lustre in the sun; her complexion was of an exquisite whiteness and with a delicate flush; the chiseling of her features was peculiarly fine, in clear, sharp lines — she was called " hatchet-faced " by her undiscriminating friends. She wore a coarse, flimsy, pink muslin dress which showed a repetitious pattern of vague green leaves, and as she flitted, lissome and swaying, through the throng, with the wind a-flutter in her full draperies, she might have suggested to a spectator the semblance of a pink flower—of the humbler varieties, perhaps, but still a wild rose is a rose.

Even the longest dance must have an end; even the stanchest mountain fiddler will reach at last his limit of endurance and must needs be refreshed and fed. There was a sudden significant flourish of frisky bowing, now up and again down, enlisting every resonant capacity of horsehair and catgut; the violins quavered to a final long-drawn scrape and silence descended. Dullness ensued; the flavor of the day seemed to pall; the dancers scattered and were presently following the crowd that began to slowly gather about the vacated stand of the musicians, from which elevation the speakers of the occasion were about to address their fellow-citizens. One of the disaffected old farmers, gruff and averse, could not refrain from administering a rebuke to Brent Kayle as crossing the expanse of saw-dust on his way to join the audience he encountered the youth in company with Valeria Clee, his recent partner.

"Ai-yi, Brent," the old man said, "the last time I seen you uns I remember well ez ye war a-settin' on the mourner's bench." For there had been a great religious revival the previous year and many had been pricked in conscience. "Ye ain't so tuk up now in contemplatin' the goodness o' God an' yer sins agin same," he pursued caustically.

Brent retorted with obvious acrimony. "I don't see no 'casion ter doubt the goodness o' God—I never war so ongrateful nohow as that comes to." He resented being thus publicly reproached, as if he were individually responsible for the iniquity of the bran dance—the scape-goat for the sins of all this merry company. Many of the whilom dancers had pressed forward, crowding up behind the old mountaineer and facing the flushed Brent and the flower-like Valeria, the faint green leaves of her muslin dress fluttering about her as her skirts swayed in the wind.

"Ye ain't so powerful afeard of the devil *now* ez ye uster was on the mourner's bench," the old man argued.

"I never war so mighty afeard of the devil," the goaded Brent broke forth angrily, for the crowd was laughing in great relish of his predicament—they, who had shared all the enormity of "shaking a foot" on this festive day. Brent flinched from the obvious injustice of their ridicule. He felt an eager impulse for reprisal. "I know ez sech dancin' ez I hev done ain't no sin," he blustered. "I ain't afeared o' the devil fur sech ez that. I wouldn't be skeered a mite ef he war ter—ter—ter speak right out now agin it, an' I'll be bound ez all o' you uns would. I—I—look yander—*look!*"

He had thrown himself into a posture of amazed intentness and was pointing upward at the overhanging boughs of a tree above their heads. A squirrel was poised thereon, gazing down motionless. Then, suddenly—a frightful thing happened. The creature seemed to speak. A strange falsetto voice, such as might befit so eerie a chance, sounded on the air—loud, distinct, heard far up the slope, and electrifying the assemblage near at hand that was gathering about the stand and awaiting the political candidates.

"Quit yer foolin'—quit yer foolin'," the strange voice iterated. "I'll larn ye ter be afeared o' the devil. Long legs now is special grace."

So wild a cry broke from the startled group below the tree that the squirrel, with a sudden, alert, about-face movement, turned and swiftly ran along the bough and up the bole. It paused once and looked back to cry out again in distinct iteration, " Quit yer foolin'! Quit yer foolin'!"

But none had stayed to listen. A general frantic rout ensued. The possibility of ventriloquism was unknown to their limited experience. All had heard the voice and those who had distinguished the words and their seeming source needed no argument. In either case the result was the same. Within ten minutes the grounds of the famous barbecue and bran dance were deserted. The cumbrous wagons, all too slow, were wending with such speed as their drivers could coerce the ox-teams to make along the woodland road homeward, while happier wights on horseback galloped past, leaving clouds of dust in the rear and a grewsome premonition of being hindmost in a flight that to the simple minds of the mountaineers had a pursuer of direful reality.

The state of a candidate is rarely enviable until the event is cast and the postulant is merged into the elect, but on the day signalized by the barbecue, the bran dance, and the rout the unfortunate aspirants for public favor felt that they had experienced the extremest spite of fate; for although they realized in their superior education and sophistication that the panic-stricken rural crowd had been tricked by some clever ventriloquist, the political orators were left with only the winds and waters and wilderness on which to waste their eloquence, and the wisdom of their exclusive method of saving the country.

Brent Kayle's talent for eluding the common doom of man to eat his bread in the sweat of his face was peculiarly marked. He was the eldest of seven sons, ranging in age from eleven to twenty years, including one pair of twins. The parents had been greatly pitied for the exorbitant exactions of rearing this large family during its immaturity, but now, the labor of farm, barnyard and woodpile, distributed among so many stalwart fellows of the same home and interest was light and the result ample. Perhaps none of them realized how little of this abundance was compassed by Brent's exertions—how many days he spent dawdling on the river bank idly experimenting with the echoes—how often, even when he affected to work, he left the plow in the furrow while he followed till sunset the flight of successive birds through the adjacent pastures, imitating as he went the fresh mid-air cry, whistling in so vibrant a bird-voice, so signally clear and dulcet, yet so keen despite its sweetness, that his brothers at the plow-handles sought in vain to distinguish between the calls of the earthling and the winged voyager of the empyreal air. None of them had ever heard of ventriloquism, so limited had been their education and experience, so sequestered was their home amidst the wilderness of the mountains. Only very gradually to Brent himself came the consciousness of his unique gift, as from imitation he progressed to causing a silent bird to seem to sing. The strangeness of the experience frightened him at first, but with each experiment he had grown more confident, more skilled, until at length he found that he could throw a singularly articulate voice into the jaws of the old plow-horse, while his brothers, accustomed to his queer vocal tricks, were convulsed with laughter at the bizarre quadrupedal views of life thus elicited. This development of proficiency, however, was recent, and until the incident at the bran dance it had not been exercised beyond the limits of their secluded home. It had revealed new possibilities to the young ventriloquist and he looked at once agitated, excited, and triumphant when late that afternoon he appeared suddenly at the rail fence about the door-yard of Valeria Clee's home on one of the spurs of Chilhowee Mountain.

It was no such home as his—lacking all the evidence of rude comfort and coarse plenty that reigned there—and in its tumble-down disrepair it had an aspect of dispirited helplessness. Here Valeria, an orphan from her infancy, dwelt with her father's parents, who always of small means had become yearly a more precarious support. The ancient grandmother was sunken in many infirmities, and the household tasks had all fallen to the lot of Valeria. Latterly a stroke of paralysis had given old man Clee an awful annotation on the chapter of age and poverty upon which he was entering, and his little farm was fast growing up in brambles.

"But 't ain't no differ, gran'dad," Valeria often sought to reassure him. "*I'll* work some way out."

And when he would irritably flout the possibility that she could do aught to materially avert disaster she was wont to protest: "You jes' watch *me*. *I'll* find out some way. I be ez knowin' ez any old *owel*."

Despite her slender physique and her recurrent heavy tasks the drear doom of poverty with its multiform menace had cast no shadow on her ethereal face, and her pensive dark gray eyes were full of serene light as she met the visitor at the bars. A glimmer of mirth began to scintillate beneath her long brown lashes, and she spoke first. "The folks in the mountings air mighty nigh skeered out'n thar boots by yer foolishness, Brent "—she sought to conserve a mien of reproof. "They 'low ez it war a manifestation of the Evil One."

Brent laughed delightedly. "Warn't

it prime?" he said. " But I never expected ter work sech a scatteration of the crowd. Thar skeer plumb tarrified *me*. I jes' set out with the nimblest, an' run from the devil myself."

"Won't them candidates fur office be mighty mad if they find out what it war sure enough?" she queried anxiously. "They gin the crowd a barbecue an' bran dance, an' arter all, the folks got quit of hevin' ter hear them speak an' jaw about thar old politics an' sech."

"Them candidates air hoppin' mad fur true," he admitted. "I been down yander at Gilfillan's store in the Cove an' I hearn the loafers thar talkin' powerful 'bout the strange happening. An' them candidates war thar gittin' ready ter start out fur town in thar buggy. An' that thar gay one—though now he seems ez sober ez that sour one—he said 't warn't no devil. 'Twar jes' a ventriloquisk from somewhar—that's jes' what that town man called it. But *I* never said nuthin'. I kep' powerful quiet."

Brent Kayle was as vain a man as ever stood in shoe leather—even in the midst of his absorption in his disclosure he could not refrain from a pause to reflect on the signal success of his prank and laugh and plume himself.

" But old Gilfillan he loves ter believe ez the devil air hotfoot arter other folks with a pitchfork, an' he axed how then did sech a man happen ter be in the mountings 'thout none knowin' of it. An' that candidate, the gay one, he say he reckon the feller kem from that circus what is goin' ter show in Shaftesville termorrer—mebbe he hearn 'bout the bran dance an' wanted ter hev some fun out'n the country folks. That candidate say he hed hearn dozens o' ventriloquisks in shows in the big towns—though this war about the bes' one he could remember. He said he hed no doubt this feller is paid good money in the show, fur jes' sech fool tricks with his voice—*good money!*"

Valeria had listened in motionless amazement. But he had now paused, almost choking with his rush of emotion, his excitement, his sense of triumph, and straight ensued a certain reluctance, a dull negation, a prophetic recoil from responsibility that clogged his resolve. His eyes roved uncertainly about the familiar domestic scene, darkening now, duskily purple beneath the luminous pearly and roseate tints of the twilight sky. The old woman was a-drowse on the porch of the rickety little log-cabin beneath the gourd vines, the paralytic grandfather came hirpling unsteadily through the doorway on his supporting crutch, his pipe shaking in his shaking hand, while he muttered and mumbled to himself—who knows what?—whether of terror of the future, or regret for the past, or doubt and despair of to-day. The place was obviously so meagre, so poverty-bitten, so eloquent of the hard struggle for mere existence. If it had been necessary for Brent Kayle to put his hand to the plow in its behalf the words would never have been spoken—but "good money" for this idle trade, these facile pranks!

"Vallie," he said impulsively, "I'm going ter try it—ef ye'll go with me. Ef ye war along I'd feel heartened ter stand up an' face the crowd in a strange place. I always loved ye better than any of the other gals—shucks!—whenst *ye* war about I never knowed ez they war alive."

Perhaps it was the after-glow of the sunset in the sky, but a crimson flush sprang into her delicate cheek; her eyes were evasive, quickly glancing here and there with an affectation of indifference, and she had no mind to talk of love, she declared.

But she should think of her gran'dad and gran'mam, he persisted. How had she the heart to deprive them of his willing aid? He declared he had intended to ask her to marry him anyhow, for she had always seemed to like him—she could not deny this—but now was the auspicious time—to-morrow— while the circus was in Shaftesville, and " good money " was to be had to provide for the wants of her old grandparents.

Though Valeria had flouted the talk of love she seemed his partisan when she confided the matter to the two old people and their consent was accorded rather for her sake than their own. They felt a revivifying impetus in the thought that after their death Valeria would have a good husband to care for her, for to them the chief grief of their loosening hold on life was her inheritance of their helplessness and poverty.

The courthouse in Shaftesville seemed a very imposing edifice to people unaccustomed to the giddy heights of a second story

UNA OF THE HILL COUNTRY

When the two staring young rustics left the desk of the county court clerk and repaired to the dwelling of the minister of the Methodist Church near by, with the marriage license just procured safely stowed away in Brent's capacious hat, their anxieties were roused for a moment lest some delay ensue, as they discovered that the minister was on the point of sitting down to his dinner. He courteously deferred the meal, however, and as the bride apologetically remarked after the ceremony that they might have awaited his convenience were it not for the circus, he imagined that the youthful couple had designed to utilize a round of the menagerie as a wedding tour. The same thought was in the minds of the metropolitan managers of the organization when presently the two young wildings from the mountain fastness were ushered into their presence, having secured an audience by dint of extreme persistence, aided by a mien of mysterious importance.

They found two men standing just within the great empty tent, for the crowd had not as yet begun to gather. The most authoritative, who was tall and portly, had the manner of swiftly disposing of the incident by asking in a peremptory voice what he could do for them. The other, lean and languid, looked up from a newspaper, in which he had been scanning a flaming circus advertisement, as he stood smoking a cigar. He said nothing, but concentrated an intent speculative gaze on the face of Valeria, who had pulled off her faint green sunbonnet and in a flush of eager hopefulness fanned with the slats.

"Ventriloquist?" the portly man repeated with a note of surprise, as Brent made known his gifts and his desire for an engagement. "Oh, well—ventriloquism is a chestnut."

Then with a qualm of pity, perhaps, for the blank despair that settled down on the two young faces he explained: "Nothing goes in the circus business but novelty. The public is tired out with ventriloquism. No mystery about it now—kind of thing, too, that a clever amateur can compass."

Brent, hurled from the giddy heights of imminent achievement to the depths of nullity, could not at once relinquish the glowing prospects that had allured him. He offered to give a sample of his powers. He would like to bark a few, he said; you couldn't tell him from a sure enough dog; he could imitate the different breeds—hound-dog, bull-pup, terrier—but the manager was definitely shaking his head.

Suddenly his partner spoke. "The girl might take a turn!"

"In the show?" the portly man said in surprise.

"The Company's Una weighs two hundred pounds and has a face as broad as a barn-door. She shows she is afraid of the lion when she stands beside him in the street parade, and—curse him— he is so clever that he knows it, no matter how he is doped. It incites him to growl at her all through the pageant, and that simply queers the sweet peace of the idea."

"And you think this untrained girl could take her place?"

"Why not? She couldn't do worse—and she *could* look the part. See," he continued, in as business-like way as if Valeria were merely a bale of goods or deaf, "ethereal figure, poetic type of beauty, fine expression of candor and serene courage. She has a look of open-eyed innocence—I don't mean *ignorance*." He made a subtle distinction in the untutored aspect of the two countenances before him.

"Would you be afraid of the lion, child?" the stout man asked Valeria. "He is chained —and drugged, too—in the pageant."

It was difficult for the astonished Valeria to find her voice. "A lion?" she murmured. "I never seen a lion."

"No? Honest?" they both cried in amazement that such a thing could be. The portly man's rollicking laughter rang out through the thin walls of canvas to such effect that some savage caged beast within reach of the elastic buoyant sound was roused to anger and supplemented it with a rancorous snarl.

Valeria listened apprehensively, with dilated eyes. She thought of the lion, the ferocious creature that she had never seen. She thought of the massive strong woman who knew and feared him. Then she remembered the desolate old grandparents and their hopeless, helpless poverty. "I'll resk the lion," she said with a tremulous bated voice.

"That's a brave girl," cried the manager.

"I hev read 'bout Daniel's lions an' him in the den," she explained. "An' Daniel hed consid'ble trust an' warn't afeard—an' mebbe I won't be afeard nuther."

"Daniel's Lions? Daniel's Lions?" the portly manager repeated attentively. "I don't know the show—perhaps in some combination now." For if he had ever heard of that signal leonine incident recorded in Scripture he had forgotten it. "Yes, yes," as Valeria eagerly appealed to him in behalf of Brent, "we must try to give Hubby some little stunt to do in the performance—but *you* are the ticket—a sure winner."

Of course the public knew, if it chose to reflect, that though apparently free the lion was muzzled with a strong steel ring, and every ponderous paw was chained down securely to the exhibition car; it may even have suspected that the savage proclivities of the great beast were dulled by drugs. But there is always the imminent chance of some failure of precaution, and the multitude must needs thrill to the spectacle of intrepidity and danger. Naught could exceed the enthusiasm that greeted this slim, graceful Una a few days later in the streets of a distant city, as clad in long draperies of fleecy white she reclined against a splendid leonine specimen, her shining golden hair hanging on her shoulders, or mingling with his tawny mane as now and again she let her soft cheek rest on his head, her luminous dark gray eyes smiling down at the cheering crowds. This speedily became the favorite feature of the pageant, and the billboards flamed with her portrait, leaning against the lion, hundreds of miles in advance of her triumphal progress.

All this unexpected success presently awoke Brent's emulation—so far he had not even "barked a few." A liberal advance on his wife's salary had quieted him for a time, but when the wonders of this new life began to grow stale—the steam-cars, the great cities, the vast country the Company traversed— he became importunate for the opportunity of display. He "barked a few" so cleverly at a concert after the performance one evening that the manager gave him a chance to throw the very considerable volume of sound he could command into the jaws of one of the lions. "Let Emperor speak to the people," he said. Forthwith he wrote a bit of rodomontade which he bade Brent memorize and had the satisfaction soon to hear from the lion-trainer, to whom was intrusted all that pertained to the exhibition of these kings of beasts, that the rehearsal was altogether satisfactory.

An immense audience was assembled in the great tent. The soaring dome of white canvas reflected the electric light with a moony lustre. The display of the three rings was in full swing. That magic atmosphere of the circus, the sense of simple festivity, the crises of thrilling expectancy, the revelation of successive wonders, the diffusive delight of a multitude not difficult to entertain —all were in evidence. Suddenly a ponderous cage was rolled in; the band was playing liltingly; the largest of the lions within the bars, a tawny monster, roused up and with head depressed and switching tail paced back and forth within the restricted limits of the cage, while the others looked out with motionless curiosity at the tiers of people. Presently with a long supple stride the gigantic, blond Norwegian trainer came lightly across the arena—a Hercules, with broad bare chest and arms, arrayed in spangled blue satin and white tights that forbade all suspicion of protective armor. At a single bound he sprang into the cage, while Brent, garbed in carnation and white, stood unheralded and unremarked close by outside among the armed attendants. There seemed no need of precaution, however, so lightly the trainer frolicked with the savage creatures. He performed wonderful acrobatic feats with them in which one hardly knew which most to admire, the agility and intrepidity of the man or the supple strength and curious intelligence of the beasts. He wrestled with them; he leaped and rolled among them; he put his head into their terrible full-fanged jaws—but before springing forth he fired his pistols loaded with blank cartridges full in their faces; for the instant the coercion of his eye was pretermitted every one treacherously bounded toward him, seeking to seize him before he could reach the door. Then Emperor, as was his wont, flung himself in baffled fury against the bars and stood erect and shook them in his wrath.

All at once, to the astonishment of the people, he spoke, voicing a plaintive panegyric on liberty and protesting his willingness to barter all the luxury of his captivity for one free hour on the desert sands.

UNA OF THE HILL COUNTRY

Surprise, absolute, unqualified, reigned for one moment. But a circus-going crowd is uncannily quick. The audience perceived a certain involuntary element of the entertainment. A storm of cat-calls ensued, hisses, roars of laughter. For the place was the city of Glaston, the Company being once more in East Tennessee, and the lion spoke the old familiar mountain dialect so easily recognizable in this locality. Even a *lapsus linguae*, "you uns," was unmistakable amidst the high-flown periods. Although the ventriloquism was appreciated, the incongruity of this countrified jargon, held in great contempt by the townfolks, discounted Emperor's majesty and he was in ludicrous eclipse.

Behind the screening canvas the portly manager raged; " How dare you make that fine lion talk like a 'hill-Billy' such as yourself —as if he were fresh caught in the Great Smoky Mountains!" he stormed at the indignant ventriloquist. The other partners in the management interfered in Brent's behalf; they feared that the proud mountaineer, resenting the contemptuous designation "hill-Billy" might withdraw from the Company, taking his wife with him, and the loss of Valeria from the pageant would be well nigh irreparable, for her ethereal and fragile beauty as Una with her lion had a perennial charm for the public. The management therefore assumed the responsibility for the linguistic disaster, having confided the rehearsal to a foreigner, for the Norwegian lion-trainer naively explained that to him it seemed that all Americans talked alike.

A course in elocution was recommended to Brent by the managers, and he fell in with this plan delightedly, but after two or three elementary bouts with the vowel sounds, long and short, consonants, sonant and surd, he concluded that mere articulation could be made as laborious as sawing wood, and he discovered that it was incompatible with his dignity to be a pupil in an art in which he had professed proficiency. Thereafter his accomplishment rusted—to the relief of the management—although he required that Valeria should be described in the advertisements as the wife of "the *celebrated ventriloquist,* Mr. Brent Kayle," thus seeking by faked notoriety to secure the sweets of fame, without the labor of achievement.

Valeria had welcomed the pacific settlement of the difficulty, because her "good money" earned in the show so brightened and beautified the evening of life for the venerable grandparents at home. For their sake she had conquered her dread of the lion in the pageant. Indeed she had found other lions in her path that she feared more—the glitter and gauds of her tinsel world, the enervating love of ease, the influence of sordid surroundings and ignoble ideals. But not one could withstand the simple goodness of the unsophisticated girl. They retreated before the power of her fireside traditions of right thinking and true living which she had learned in her humble mountain home.

It had come to be a dwelling of comfortable aspect, cared for in the absence of the young couple by a thrifty hired housekeeper, a widowed cousin, and here they spent the off-seasons when the circus company went into winter quarters. Repairs had been instituted, several rooms were added, and a wide veranda replaced the rickety little porch and gave upon a noble prospect of mountain and valley and river. Here on sunshiny noons in the good Saint Martin's summer the old gran'dad loved to sit, blithe and hearty, chirping away the soft unseasonable December days. Sometimes in the plenitude of content he would give Valeria a meaning glance and mutter "Oh, leetle *Owel!* Oh, leetle *Owel!*" and then break into laughter that must needs pause to let him wipe his eyes.

"Yes, Vallie 'pears ter hev right good sense an' makes out toler'ble well, considerin'," her husband would affably remark, "though of course it war *me* ez interduced her ter the managers, an' she gits her main chance in the show through my bein' a celebrated ventriloquisk."

THE LOST GUIDON

Night came early. It might well seem that day had fled affrighted. The heavy masses of clouds, glooming low, which had gathered thicker and thicker, as if crowding to witness the catastrophe, had finally shaken asunder in the concussions of the air at the discharges of artillery, and now the direful rain, always sequence of the shock of battle, was steadily falling, falling, on the stricken field. Many a soldier who might have survived his wounds would succumb to exposure to the elements during the night, debarred the tardy succor that must needs await his turn. One of the surgeons at their hasty work at the field hospital, under the shelter of the cliffs on the slope, paused to note the presage of doom and death, and to draw a long breath before he adjusted himself anew to the grim duties of the scalpel in his hand. His face was set and haggard, less with a realization of the significance of the scene—for he was used to its recurrence—than simply with a physical reflection of horror, as if it were glassed in a mirror. A phenomenon that had earlier caught his attention

THE LOST GUIDON

in the landscape appealed again to his notice, perhaps because the symptom was not in his line.

"Looks like a case of dementia," he observed to the senior surgeon, standing near at hand.

The superior officer adjusted his field-glass. "Looks like 'Death on the White Horse'!" he responded.

Down the highway, at a slow pace, rode a cavalryman wearing a gray uniform, with a sergeant's chevrons, and mounted on a steed good in his day, but whose day was gone. A great clot of blood had gathered on his broad white chest, where a bayonet had thrust him deep. Despite his exhaustion, he moved forward at the urgency of his rider's heel and hand. The soldier held a long, heavy staff planted on one stirrup, from the top of which drooped in the dull air the once gay guidon, battle-rent and sodden with rain, and as he went he shouted at intervals, "Dovinger's Rangers! Rally on the guidon!" Now and again his strident boyish voice varied the appeal, "Hyar's yer Dovinger's Rangers! Rally, boys! Rally on the reserve!"

Indeed, despite his stalwart, tall, broad-shouldered frame, he was scarcely more than a boy. His bare head had flaxen curls like a child's; his pallid, though sunburned face was broad and soft and beardless; his large blue eyes were languid and spiritless, though now and then as he turned an intent gaze over the field they flared anew with hope, as if he expected to see rise up from that desolate expanse, from among the stiffening carcasses of horses and the stark corpses of the troopers, that gallant squadron wont to follow, so dashing and debonair, wherever the guidons might mark the way. But there was naught astir save the darkness slipping down by slow degrees—and perchance under its cloak, already stealthily afoot, the ghoulish robbers of the dead that haunt the track of battle. They were the human forerunners of the vulture breed, with even a keener scent for prey, for as yet the feathered carrion-seekers held aloof; two or three only were descried from the field hospital, perched on the boughs of a dead tree near the river, presently joined by another, its splendid sustained flight impeded somewhat by the rain, battling with its big, strong wings

THE LOST GUIDON

against the downpour of the torrents and the heavy air.

And still through all echoed the cry, "Rally on the guidon! Dovinger's Rangers! Rally on the reserve!"

The bridge that crossed the river, which was running full and foaming, had been burnt; but a span, charred and broken, still swung from the central pier. Over toward the dun-tinted west a house was blazing, fired by some stray bomb, perhaps, or by official design, to hinder the enemy from utilizing the shelter, and its red rage of destruction bepainted the clouds that hung so low above the chimneys and dormer-windows. To the east, the woods on the steeps had been shelled, and a myriad boughs and boles riven and rent, lay in fantastic confusion. Through the mournful chaos the wind had begun to sweep; it sounded in unison with the battle clamors, and shrieked and wailed and roared as it surged adown the defiles. Now and then there came on the blast the fusillade of dropping shots from the south, where the skirmish line of one faction engaged the rear-guard of the other, or the pickets fell within rifle-range. Once the sullen, melancholy boom of distant

THE LOST GUIDON

cannon shook the clouds, and then was still, and ever and again sounded that tireless cry, "Dovinger's Rangers. Hyar's yer guidon! Rally, boys! Rally on the guidon! Rally on the reserve!"

The senior surgeon, as the road wound near, stepped down toward it when the horseman, still holding himself proudly erect, passed by. "Sergeant," he hailed the guidon, "where is Captain Dovinger?"

The hand mechanically went to the boy's forehead in the usual military salute. "Killed, sir."

"Where are the other officers of the squadron—the junior captain, the lieutenants?"

"Killed, sir."

"What has become of the troopers?"

"Killed, sir, in the last charge."

There was a pause. Then Dr. **Trent** broke forth: "Are you a fool, boy? If your command is annihilated, why do you keep up this commotion?"

The young fellow looked blank for a moment. Then, as if he had not reasoned on the catastrophe: "I thought at first they mought be scattered—some of 'em. But ef— ef—they *war* dead, but could once *see* the guidon, sure 't would call 'em to life. They *couldn't* be so dead but they would rally to the guidon! Guide right!" he shouted suddenly. "Dovinger's Rangers! Rally on the guidon, boys! Rally on the reserve!"

It was a time that hardened men's hearts. The young soldier had no physical hurt that might appeal to the professional sympathies of the senior surgeon, and he turned away with a half laugh. "Let him go along! He can't rally Dovinger's Rangers this side of the river Styx, it seems."

But an old chaplain who had been hovering about the field hospital, whispering a word here and there to stimulate the fortitude of the wounded and solace the fears of the dying, recognized moral symptoms alien to any diagnosis of which the senior surgeon was capable. The latter did not deplore the diversion of interest, for the old man's presence was not highly esteemed by the hospital corps at this scene of hasty and terrible work, although, having taken a course in medicine in early life, he was permitted to aid in certain ways. But the surgeons were wont to declare that the men began to bleat at the very sight of the chaplain. So gentle, so sympathetic, so paternal, was he that they made the more of their wretched woes, seeing them so deeply deplored. The senior surgeon, moreover, was not an ardent religionist. "This is no time for a revival, Mr. Whitmel," he would insist. "Jack, there, never spoke the name of God in his life, except to swear by it. He is too late for prayers, and if *I* can't pull him through, he is a goner!"

But the chaplain was fond of quoting:

"Between the stirrup and the ground
He mercy sought and mercy found——"

and sometimes the scene was irreverently called a "love feast" when some hard-riding, hard-swearing, hard-fighting, unthinking sinner went joyfully out of this world from the fatherly arms of the chaplain into the paternal embrace of an eternal and merciful Father, as the man of God firmly believed.

He stood now, staring after the guidon borne through the rain and the mist, flaunting red as the last leaves of autumn against the dun-tinted dusk, that the dead might view the gallant and honored pennant and rise again to its leading!

THE LOST GUIDON

No one followed but the tall, thin figure of the gaunt old chaplain, unless indeed the trooping shadows that kept him company had mysteriously roused at the stirring summons. Lanterns were now visible, dimly flickering in one quarter where the fighting had been furious and the slain lay six deep on the ground. Their aspirations, their valor, their patriotism, had all exhaled— volatile essences, these incomparable values! —and now their bodies, weighted with death, cumbered the earth. They must be hurried out of sight, out of remembrance soon, and the burial parties were urged to diligence at the trenches where these cast-off semblances were to lie undistinguished together. And still the reflection of the burning house reddened the gloomy west, and still the cry, "Rally on the guidon! Dovinger's Rangers!" smote the thick air.

Suddenly it was silent. The white horse that had been visible in the flare from the flaming house, now and again flung athwart the landscape, no longer loomed in the vista of the shadowy road. He had given way at last, sinking down with that martial figure still in the saddle, and, with no struggle save

THE LOST GUIDON

a mere galvanic shiver, passing away from the scene of his faithful devoirs.

Fatigue, agitation, anguish, his agonized obsession of the possibility of rallying the squadron, had served to prostrate the soldier's physical powers of resistance. He could not constrain his muscles to rise from the recumbent position against the carcass. He started up, then sank back, and in another moment triumphant nature conquered, and he was asleep—a dull, dreamless sleep of absolute exhaustion, that perchance rescued his reason as well as saved his life.

The old chaplain was a man of infinite prejudice, steeped in all the infirmities and fantasies of dogma; a lover of harmony, and essentially an apostle of peace. Nevertheless, it would not have been physically safe to call him a Jesuit. But indeed he scarcely hesitated; he stepped over the great inert bulk of the dead horse, unclenched the muscular grasp of the soldier, as if it had been a baby's clasp, slipped the staff, technically the lance, of the guidon from its socket, and stood with it in his own hand, looking suspiciously to and fro to descry if perchance he were observed. The coast clear, he turned

THE LOST GUIDON

to the wall of rock beside the road, for this was near the mountain sandstone formation, fissured, splintered, with the erosions of water and weather; and into one of the cellular, tunnel-like apertures he ran the guidon, lance and all,—lost forever from human sight.

In those days one might speak indeed of the march of events. Each seemed hard on the heels of its precursor. Change ran riot in the ordering of the world, and its aspect was utterly transformed when Casper Girard, no longer bearing the guidon of Dovinger's Rangers, came out of the war with a captain's shoulder-straps, won by personal fitness often proved, the habit of command, and a great and growing opinion of himself. He was a changeling, so to speak. No longer he felt a native of the mountain cove where he had been born and reared. He had had a glimpse of the world from a different standpoint, and it lured him. A dreary, disaffected life he led for a time.

" 'Minds me of a wild tur-r-key in a trap," his mother was wont to comment. "Always stretchin' his neck an' lookin' up an' away—when he mought git out by lookin'

THE LOST GUIDON

down." And the simile was so apt that it stayed in his mind—looking up and away!

Of all dull inventions, in his estimation the art of printing exceeded. He had made but indifferent progress in education during his early youth; he was a slow and inexpert reader, and a writer whose chirography shrank from exhibition. Now, however, a book in the hand gave him a cherished sentiment of touch with the larger world beyond those blue ranges that limited his sphere, and he spent much time in sedulously reading certain volumes which he had brought home with him.

"Spent *money* fur 'em!" his mother would ejaculate, contemplating this extreme audacity of extravagance.

As she often observed, "the plough-handles seemed red-hot," and as soon as political conditions favored he ran for office. On the strength of his war record, a potent lever in those days, he was elected register of the county. True, there was only a population of about fifty souls in the county town, and the houses were log-cabins, except the temple of justice itself, which was a two-story frame building. But his success was a step

THE LOST GUIDON

on the road to political preferment, and his ambitious eyes were on the future. Into the midst of his quiet incumbency as register came Fate, all intrusive, and found him through the infrequent medium of a weekly mail. It was at the beginning of the retrospective enthusiasm that has served to revive the memories of the War, and he received a letter from an old comrade-in-arms, giving the details of a brigade reunion shortly to be held at no great distance, and, being of the committee, inviting him to be present.

Girard had participated in great military crises; he had marshalled his troop in line of battle; as a mere boy, he had ridden with the guidon lance planted on his stirrup, with the pennant flying above his head, as the marker to lead the fierce and famous Dovinger Rangers into the thickest of the fight; yet he had never felt such palpitant tremors of excitement as when he stood on the hotel piazza of the New Helvetia Springs, where the banqueters had gathered, and suffered the ordeal of introduction to sundry groups of fashionable ladies. He had earlier seen specimens of the species in the course of military transitions through the cities of the lowlands, and he watched them narrowly to detect if they discerned perchance a difference between him and the men of education and social station with whom his advancement in the army had associated him. He did not reflect that they were too well-bred to reveal any appreciation of such incongruity, but he had never experienced a more ardent glow of gratification than upon overhearing a friend's remark: "Girard is great! Anybody would imagine he was used to all this!"

No strategist was ever more wary. He would not undertake to dance, for he readily perceived that the gyrations in the ball-room were utterly dissimilar to the clumsy capering to which he had been accustomed on the puncheon floor of a mountain cabin. He had the less reason for regret since he was privileged instead to stroll up and down the veranda,—"promenade" was the technical term,—a slender hand, delicately gloved, on the sleeve of his gray uniform, the old regimentals being *de rigueur* at these reunions. A white ball-gown, such as he had never before seen, fashioned of tissue over lustrous white silk, swayed in diaphanous folds against him, for these were the days of voluminous draperies; a head of auburn hair elaborately dressed gleamed in the moonlight near his shoulder. Miss Alicia Duval thought him tremendously handsome; she adored his record, as she would have said—unaware how little of it she knew—and she did not so much intend to flirt as to draw him out, for there was something about him different from the men of her set, and it stimulated her interest.

"Isn't the moon heavenly?" she observed, gazing at the brilliant orb, now near the full, swinging in the sky, which became a definite blue in its light above the massive dark mountains and the misty valley below; for the building was as near the brink as safety permitted—nearer, the cautious opined.

"Heavenly? Not more'n it's got a right to be. It's a heavenly body, ain't it?" he rejoined.

"Oh, how sarcastic!" she exclaimed. "In what school did you acquire your trenchant style?"

He thought of the tiny district school where he had acquired the very little he knew of aught, and said nothing, laughing constrainedly in lieu of response.

THE LOST GUIDON

The music of the orchestra came to them from the ball-room, and the rhythmic beat of dancing feet; the wind lifted her hair gently and brought to them the fragrance of flowering plants and the pungent aroma of mint down in the depths of the ravine hard by, where lurked a chalybeate spring; but for the noisy rout of the dance, and now and again the flimsy chatter of a passing couple on the piazza, promenading like themselves, they might have heard the waters of the fountain rise and bubble and break and sigh as the pulsating impulse beat like heart-throbs, and perchance on its rocky marge an oread a-singing.

"But you don't answer me," she pouted with an affectation of pettishness. "Do you know that you trouble yourself to talk very little, Captain Girard?"

"I think the more," he declared.

"Think? Oh, dear me! I didn't know that anybody does anything so unfashionable nowadays as to *think!* And what do you think about, pray?"

"About you!"

And that began it: he was a gallant man, and he had been a brave one. He was not aware how far he was going on so short an acquaintance, but his temerity was not displeasing to the lady. She liked his manner of storming the citadel, and she did not realize that he merely spoke at random, as best he might. He was in his uniform a splendid and martial presentment of military youth, and indeed he was much the junior of his compeers.

"Who are Captain Girard's people, Papa?" she asked Colonel Duval next morning, as the family party sat at breakfast in quasi seclusion at one of the small round tables in the crowded dining-room, full of the chatter of people and the clatter of dishes.

"Girard?" Colonel Duval repeated thoughtfully. "I really don't know. I have an impression they live somewhere in East Tennessee. I never met him till just about the end of the war."

"Oh, Papa! How unsatisfactory you are! You never know anything about anybody."

"I should think his people must be very plain," said Mrs. Duval. Her social discrimination was extremely acute and in constant practice.

"I don't know why. He is very much of

a gentleman," the Colonel contended. His heart was warm to-day with much fraternizing, and it was not kind to brush the bloom off his peach.

"Oh, trifles suggest the fact. He is not at all *au fait*."

He was, however, experienced in ways of the world unimagined in her philosophy. The reunion had drawn to a close, ending in a flare of jollity and tender reminiscence and good-fellowship. The old soldiers were all gone save a few regular patrons of the hotel, who with their families were completing their summer sojourn. Captain Girard lingered, too, fascinated by this glimpse of the frivolous world, hitherto unimagined, rather than by the incense to his vanity offered by his facile acceptance as a squire of dames. For the first time in his life he felt the grinding lack of money. Being a man of resource, he set about swiftly supplying this need. In the dull days of inaction, when the armies lay supine and only occasionally the monotony was broken by the engagement of distant skirmishers or a picket line was driven in on the main body, he had learned to play a game at cards much in vogue at that period,

THE LOST GUIDON

though for no greater hazards than grains of corn or Confederate money, almost as worthless. In the realization now that the same principles held good with stakes of value, he seemed to enter upon the possession of a veritable gold mine. The peculiar traits that his one unique experience of the world had developed—his coolness, his courage, his discernment of strategic resources—stood him in good stead, and long after the microcosm of the hotel lay fast asleep the cards were dealt and play ran high in the little building called the casino, ostensibly devoted to the milder delights of billiards and cigars.

Either luck favored him or he had rare discrimination of relative chances in the run of the cards, or the phenomenally bold hand he played disconcerted his adversaries, but his almost invariable winning began to affect injuriously his character. Indeed, he was said to be a rook of unrivalled rapacity. Colonel Duval was in the frame of mind that his wife called "bearish" one morning as his family gathered for breakfast in the limited privacy of their circle about the round table in the dining-room.

"I want you to avoid that fellow, Alicia,"

he growled *sotto voce,* as he intercepted a bright matutinal smile that the fair Alicia sent as a morning greeting to Girard, who had just entered and taken his seat at a distance. "We know nothing under heaven about his people, and he himself has the repute of being a desperate gambler."

His wife raised significant eyebrows. "If that is true, why should he stay in this quiet place?"

Colonel Duval experienced a momentary embarrassment. "Oh, the place is right enough. He stays, no doubt, because he likes it. You might as well ask why old Mr. Whitmel stays here."

"The idea of mentioning a clergyman in this connection!"

"Mr. Whitmel is professionally busy," cried Alicia. "He told me that he is studying 'the disintegration of a soul.' I hope it is not *my* soul."

The phrase probably interested Alicia in her idleness, for she was certainly actuated by no view of a moral uplift in the character of Girard, the handsome gambler. She did not recognize a subtle cruelty in her system

THE LOST GUIDON

of universal fascination, but her vanity demanded constant tribute, and she was peculiarly absorbed in the effort to bring to her feet this man of iron, her knight in armor, as she was wont to call him, to control him with her influence, to bend this unmalleable material like the proverbial wax in her hands. She had great faith in the coercive power of her hazel eyes, and she brought their batteries to bear on Girard on the first occasion when she had him at her mercy.

"I have heard something about you which is very painful," she said one day as they sat together beside the chalybeate spring. The crag, all discolored in rust-red streaks by the dripping of the mineral water through its interstices, towered above their heads; the ferns, exquisite and of subtle fragrance, tufted the niches; the trees were close about them, and below, on the precipitous slope; sometimes the lush green boughs parted, revealing a distant landscape of azure ranges, far stretching against a sky as blue, and in the valley of the foreground long bars of golden hue, where fields, denuded of the harvested wheat, took the sun. Girard lounged, languid, taciturn, and quiescent as ever, on the opposite side of the circular rock basin wherein the clear water fell.

"I will tell you what it is," Alicia went on, after a pause, for, though he looked attentive, he gave not even a glance of question. "I hear that you gamble."

His gaze concentrated as he knitted his brows, but he said nothing.

She pulled her broad straw hat forward on her auburn hair and readjusted the flounces of her white morning dress, saying while thus engaged, "Yes, indeed; that you gamble—like—like fury!"

"Why, don't you know that's against the law?" he demanded unexpectedly.

"I know that it is very wrong and sinful," she said solemnly.

"Thanky. I'll put that in my pipe an' smoke it! I'm very wrong and sinful, I am given to understand."

"Why, I didn't mean *you* so much," she faltered, perturbed by this sudden charge of the enemy. "I meant the practice."

"Oh, I know that I'm a sinner in more ways 'n one; but I *didn't* know that you were a lady-preacher."

THE LOST GUIDON

"You mean that it is none of my business——"

"You ought to be so glad of that," he retorted.

She maintained a silence that might have suggested a degree of offended pride, and she was truly humiliated that her vaunted hazel eyes had so signally failed to work their wonted charm. As they strolled back together up the steep path to the hotel he seemed either unobservant or uncaring, so impassive were his manners, and she was aware that her demonstration had resulted in giving him information which he could not otherwise have gained. Later, she was nettled to notice that he had utilized it in prosaic fashion, for that night no lights flared late from the casino.

The gamesters, informed that rumors were a-wing, had betaken themselves elsewhere. A small smoking-room in the hotel proper seemed less obnoxious to suspicion in the depleted condition of the guest-list, since autumn was now approaching. After eleven o'clock the coterie would scarcely be subject to interruption, and there they gathered as the hour waxed late. The cards were duly dealt, the draw was on, when suddenly the door opened and old Mr. Whitmel, his favorite meerschaum in his hand and a sheaf of newly arrived journals, entered with the evident intention of a prolonged stay. A "standpatter" seemed hardly so assured as before he encountered the dim, surprised gaze, but the old clergyman was esteemed a good sort, and he ventured on a reminder:

"You have been here before, haven't you, Mr. Whitmel? Saw a deal of this sort of thing in the army!" And he rattled the chips significantly.

"Used to see that sort of thing in the army? Yes, yes, indeed—more than I wanted to see—very much more!"

Colonel Duval took schooling much amiss. He turned up his florid face with its auburn mustachios and Burnside whiskers from its bending over the cards and showed a broad arch of glittering white teeth in an ungenial laugh.

"Remember, Mr. Whitmel, at that fight we had in the hills not far from the Ocoee, how you rebuked two artillerymen for swearing? Something was wrong with the vent-hole of the piece, and one of the gunners asked what business you had with their language; and you said, 'I am a minister of the Lord,' and the fellow gave it back very patly, 'I ain't carin' ef you was a minister of state!' Then you said, 'No, you would doubtless swear in the presence of an angel.' And the fellow with the sponge-staff declared, 'Say, Mister, ef you are *that,* you are an angel off your feed certain'—you were worn to skin and bone then—'an' the rations of manna must be ez skimpy in heaven ez the rations o' bacon down here in Dixie.' Ha, ha, ha!''

Mr. Whitmel had taken a seat in an easy-chair; he had struck a match and was composedly kindling his pipe. "I felt nearer a higher communion that day than often since," he said.

The coterie of gentlemen looked at one another in disconsolate uncertainty, and one turned his cards face downward and laid them resignedly on the table. The party was evidently in for one of the old chaplain's long stories, with a few words by way of application, and there was no decent opportunity to demur. They were the intruders in the smoking-room—not he! Here with his pipe and his paper, he was within the accommoda-

THE LOST GUIDON

tion assigned him. They must hie them back to the casino to be at ease, and this would they do when he should reach the end of his story—if indeed it had an end.

For with the prolixity of the eye-witness he was detailing the points of the battle; what troops were engaged; how the flank was turned; how the reserve was delayed; how the guns were planted; how the cavalry was ordered to charge over impracticable ground, and how in consequence he saw a squadron literally annihilated; how for hours after the fight was over a sergeant of the Dovinger Rangers pervaded the field with the guidon, calling on them by name to rally.

"And, gentlemen," he continued, turning in his chair, the fire kindling in his eyes as it died in the bowl of his pipe, "not one man responded, for none could rise from that horrid slaughter."

There was a moment of tense silence. Then, "Back and forth the guidon flaunted, and the rain began to fall, and the night came on, and still the dusk echoed the cry, 'Guide right! Dovinger's Rangers! Rally on the guidon! Rally on the reserve!'"

The old chaplain stuck his pipe into his

THE LOST GUIDON

mouth and brought it aflare again with two or three strong indrawing respirations.

"The surgeons said it would end in a case of dementia. I was sorry, for I had seen much that day that hurt me, and more than all was this. For I could picture that valiant young spirit going through life, spared by God's mercy; and it seemed to me that when the enemy, in whatever guise, should press him hard and defeat should bear him down he would have the courage and the ardor and the moral strength to rally on the reserve. He would rally on the guidon."

The old chaplain pulled strongly at his pipe, setting the blue wreaths of smoke circling about his head. "I should know that young fellow again wherever I might chance to see him."

"Did he collapse at last and verify the surgeon's prophecy?" asked the dealer.

"Well," drawled the chaplain, with a little flattered laugh, "I myself took care of that. Many years ago I studied medicine, before I was favored with a higher call. Neurology was my line. When the boy's horse sank exhausted beneath him, and he fell into a sleep or stupor on the carcass, I removed the object

THE LOST GUIDON

of the obsession. I slipped the flag-staff, guidon and all, into a crevice of the rocks, where it will remain till the end of our time, be sure." He laughed in relish of his arbitrary intervention.

"There was a fine healthy clamor in camp the next morning about the lost guidon. But I did the soldier no damage, for he had been promoted to a lieutenancy for special gallantry on the field, and he therefore could no longer have carried the guidon if he had had both the flag and the troop."

The stories of camp and field, thus begun, swiftly multiplied; they wore the fire to embers, and the oil sank low in the lamps. There was a chill sense of dawn in the blue-gray mist when the group, separating at last, issued upon the veranda; the moon, so long hovering over the sombre massive mountains, was slowly sinking in the west.

Among the shadows of the pillars a tall, martial figure lurked in ambush for the old chaplain, as he rounded the corner of the veranda on his way to his own quarters.

"Pa'son," a husky voice spoke from out the dim comminglement of the mist and the moon, " 'twas me that carried that guidon in Dovinger's Rangers."

"I know it," declared the triumphant tactician. "I recognized you as soon as I saw you again."

"I'm through with this," the young mountaineer exclaimed abruptly, with an eloquent gesture of renunciation toward the deserted card-table visible through the vista of open doors. "I'm going home—to work! I'll never forget that I was marker in Dovinger's Rangers. I carried the guidon! And that last day I marked their way to glory! There's nothing left of them except honor and duty, but I'll rally on that, Chaplain. Never fear for me, again. I'll rally on the reserve!"

WOLF'S HEAD

It might well be called the country of the outlaw, this vast tract of dense mountain forests and craggy ravines, this congeries of swirling torrents and cataracts and rapids. Here wild beasts lurked out their savage lives, subsisting by fang and prey,—the panther, the bear, the catamount, the wolf,—and like unto them, ferocious and fugitive, both fearsome and afraid, the man with a "wolf's head," on which was set a price, even as the State's bounty for the scalps of the ravening brutes.

One gloomy October afternoon, the zest of a group of sportsmen, who had pitched their camp in this sequestered wilderness, suffered an abatement on the discovery of the repute of the region and the possibility of being summoned to serve on a sheriff's posse in the discharge of the grimmest of duties.

"But he is no outlaw in the proper sense of the term. The phrase has survived, but the fact is obsolete," said Seymour, who was both a prig and a purist, a man of leisure, and bookish, but a good shot, and vain of his sylvan accomplishments. "Our law places no man beyond the pale of its protection. He has a constitutional right to plead his case in court."

"What is the reward offered to hale him forth and force him to enjoy that privilege—five hundred dollars?" asked Bygrave, who was a newspaper man and had a habit of easy satire.

"Of course he would never suffer himself to be taken alive." Purcell's vocation was that of a broker, and he was given to the discrimination of chances and relative values. "Therefore he is as definitely *caput lupinum* as any outlaw of old. Nobody would be held accountable for cracking his 'wolf's head' off, in the effort to arrest him for the sake of the five hundred dollars. But, meantime, how does the fellow contrive to live?"

"Jes by his rifle, I reckon," replied the rural gossip whom intrusive curiosity occasionally lured to their camp-fire. "Though sence that thar big reward hev been n'ised abroad, I'd think he'd be plumb afraid ter fire a shot. The echoes be mighty peart these dumb, damp fall days."

WOLF'S HEAD

The old jeans-clad mountaineer had a certain keen spryness of aspect, despite his bent knees and stooped shoulders. His deeply grooved, narrow, thin face was yet more elongated by the extension of a high forehead into a bald crown, for he wore his broad wool hat on the back of his head. There was something in his countenance not dissimilar to the facial contour of a grasshopper, and the suggestion was heightened by his persistent, rasping chirp.

"That's what frets Meddy; she can't abide the idee of huntin' a human with sech special coursers ez money reward. She 'lows it mought tempt a' evil man or a' ignorunt one ter swear a miser'ble wretch's life away. Let the law strengthen its own hands—that's what Meddy say. Don't kindle the sperit of Cain in every brother's breast. Oh, Meddy is plumb comical whenst she fairly gits ter goin', though it's all on account of that thar man what war growed up in a tree."

The dryadic suggestions of a dendroidal captivity flashed into Seymour's mind with the phrase, and stimulated his curiosity as to some quaint rural perversion of the legend.

WOLF'S HEAD

But it was grim fact that the old mountaineer detailed in answer to the question, as he sat on a log by the fire, while the sportsmen lay on the ground about it and idly listened.

"One day—'t war 'bout two year' ago— thar war a valley-man up hyar a-huntin' in the mountings with some other fellers, an' toward sunset he war a-waitin' at a stand on a deer-path up thar nigh Headlong Creek, hopin' ter git a shot whenst the deer went down to drink. Waal, I reckon luck war ag'in' him, fer he got nuthin' but durned tired. So, ez he waited, he grounded his rifle, an' leaned himself ag'in' a great big tree ter rest his bones. And presently he jes happened ter turn his head, an', folks! he seen a sight! Fer thar, right close ter his cheek, he looked into a skellington's eye-sockets. Thar war a skellington's grisly face peerin' at him through a crack in the bark."

The raconteur suddenly stopped short, while the group remained silent in expectancy. The camp-fire, with its elastic, leaping flames, had bepainted the darkening avenues of the russet woods with long, fibrous strokes of red and yellow, as with a brush scant of color. The autumnal air was dank, with subtle shivers. A precipice was not far distant on the western side, and there the darksome forest fell away, showing above the massive, purple mountains a section of sky in a heightened clarity of tint, a suave, saffron hue, with one horizontal bar of vivid vermilion that lured the eye. The old mountaineer gazed retrospectively at it as he resumed:

"Waal, sirs, that town-man had never consorted with sech ez skellingtons. He lit out straight! He made tracks! He never stopped till he reached Colbury, an' thar he told his tale. Then the sheriff he tuk a hand in the game. Skellingtons, he said, didn't grow on trees spontaneous, an' he hed an official interes' in human relics out o' place. So he kem,—the tree is 'twixt hyar an' my house thar on the rise,—an', folks! the tale war plain. Some man chased off'n the face of the yearth, hid out from the law,—that's the way Meddy takes it,—he hed clomb the tree, an' it bein' holler, he drapped down inside it, thinkin' o' course he could git out the way he went in. But, no! It mought hev been deeper 'n he calculated, or mo' narrow, but he couldn't make the rise. He died still strugglin', fer his long, bony fingers war gripped in the wood—it's rotted a deal sence then."

"Who was the man?" asked Seymour.

"Nobody knows,—nobody keers 'cept' Meddy. She hev wep' a bushel o' tears about him. The cor'ner 'lowed from the old-fashioned flint-lock rifle he hed with him that it mus' hev happened nigh a hunderd years ago. Meddy she will git ter studyin' on that of a winter night, an' how the woman that keered fer him mus' hev watched an' waited fer him, an' 'lowed he war deceitful an' desertin', an' mebbe held a gredge agin him, whilst he war dyin' so pitiful an' helpless, walled up in that tree. Then Meddy will tune up agin, an' mighty nigh cry her eyes out. He warn't even graced with a death-bed ter breathe his last; Meddy air partic'lar afflicted that he hed ter die afoot." Old Kettison glanced about the circle, consciously facetious, his heavily grooved face distended in a mocking grin.

"A horrible fate!" exclaimed Seymour, with a half-shudder.

"Edzac'ly," the old mountaineer assented easily.

"What's her name—Meggy?" asked the journalist, with a mechanical aptitude for detail, no definite curiosity.

"Naw; Meddy—short fer Meddlesome. Her right name is Clementina Haddox; but I reckon every livin' soul hev forgot' it but me. She is jes Meddlesome by name, an' meddlesome by natur'."

He suddenly turned, gazing up the steep, wooded slope with an expectant mien, for the gentle rustling amidst the dense, red leaves of the sumac-bushes heralded an approach.

"That mus' be Meddy now," he commented, "with her salt-risin' bread. She 'lowed she war goin' ter fetch you-uns some whenst I tol' her you-uns war lackin'."

For the camp-hunt had already been signalized by divers disasters: the store of loaves in the wagon had been soaked by an inopportune shower; the young mountaineer who had combined the offices of guide and cook was the victim of an accidental discharge of a fowling-piece, receiving a load of bird-shot full in his face. Though his injury was slight, he had returned home, promising to supply his place by sending his brother, who had not yet arrived. Purcell's boast that he could bake ash-cake proved a bluff, and although the party could and did broil bacon and even birds on the coals, they were reduced to the extremity of need for the staff of life.

Hence they were predisposed in the ministrant's favor as she appeared, and were surprised to find that Meddlesome, instead of masterful and middle-aged, was a girl of eighteen, looking very shy and appealing as she paused on the verge of the flaring sumac copse, one hand lifted to a swaying bough, the other arm sustaining a basket. Even her coarse gown lent itself to pleasing effect, since its dull-brown hue composed well with the red and russet glow of the leaves about her, and its short waist, close sleeves, and scant skirt, reaching to the instep, the immemorial fashion of the hills, were less of a grotesque rusticity since there was prevalent elsewhere a vogue of quasi-Empire modes, of which the cut of her garb was reminiscent. A saffron kerchief about her throat had in its folds a necklace of over-cup acorns in three strands, and her hair, meekly parted on her forehead, was of a lustrous brown, and fell in heavy undulations on her shoulders. There was a delicate but distinct tracery of blue veins in her milky-white complexion, and she might have seemed eminently calculated for meddling disastrously with the peace of mind of the mountain youth were it not for the preoccupied expression of her eyes. Though large, brown and long-lashed, they were full of care and perplexity, and a frowning, disconcerted line between her eye-brows was so marked as almost to throw her face out of drawing. Troubled about many things, evidently, was Meddlesome. She could not even delegate the opening of a basket that her little brother had brought and placed beside the camp-fire.

"Don't, Gran'dad," she exclaimed suddenly, stepping alertly forward—"*don't* put that loaf in that thar bread-box; the box 'pears ter be damp. Leave the loaf in the big basket till ter-morrer. It'll eat shorter then, bein' fraish-baked. They kin hev these biscuits fer supper,"—dropping on one knee and setting forth on the cloth, from the basket on her arm, some thick soggy-looking lumps of dough,—"I baked some dodgers, too— four, six, eight, ten,"—she was counting a dozen golden-brown cates of delectable aspect —"knowin' they would hone fer cornmeal arter huntin', an' nuthin' else nohow air fitten ter eat with feesh or aigs. Hev you-uns got any aigs?" She sprang up, and, standing on agile tiptoe, peered without ceremony into their wagon. Instantly she recoiled with a cry of horrified reproach. "Thar 's ants in yer short-sweetenin'! How *could* you-uns let sech ez that happen?"

"Oh, surely not," exclaimed Purcell, hastening to her side. But the fact could not be gainsaid; the neglected sugar was spoiled.

Meddlesome's unwarranted intrusion into the arcana of their domestic concerns disclosed other shortcomings. "Why n't ye keep the top on yer coffee-can? Don't ye know the coffee will lose heart, settin' open?" She repaired this oversight with a deft touch, and then proceeded: "We-uns ain't got no short-sweetenin' at our house, but I'll send my leetle brother ter fetch some long-sweetenin' fer yer coffee ter night. Hyar, Sol," —addressing the small, limber, tow-headed, barefooted boy, a ludicrous miniature of a man in long, loose, brown-jeans trousers supported by a single suspender over an unbleached cotton shirt,—"run ter the house an' fetch the sorghum-jug."

As Sol started off with the alertness of

a scurrying rabbit, she shrilly called out in a frenzy of warning: "Go the other way, Sol—up through the pawpaws! Them cherty rocks will cut yer feet like a knife."

Sol had nerves of his own. Her sharp cry had caused him to spring precipitately backward, frightened, but uncomprehending his danger. Being unhurt, he was resentful. "They ain't none o' *yer* feet, nohow," he grumbled, making a fresh start at less speed.

"Oh, yes, Sol," said the old grandfather, enjoying the contretemps and the sentiment of revolt against Meddlesome's iron rule. "Everything belongs ter Meddlesome one way or another, 'ca'se she jes makes it hern. So take keer of *yer* feet for *her* sake." He turned toward her jocosely as the small emissary disappeared among the undergrowth. "I jes been tellin' these hunter-men, Meddy, 'bout how ye sets yerself even ter meddle with other folkses' mournin',—what they got through with a hunderd year' ago—tormentatin' 'bout that thar man what war starved in the tree."

She heard him, doubtless, for a rising flush betokened her deprecation of this ridicule in the presence of these strangers. But it was rather that she remembered his words afterward than heeded them now. It would seem that certain incidents, insignificant in themselves, are the pivots on which turns the scheme of fate. She could not imagine that upon her action in the next few seconds depended grave potentialities in more lives than one. On the contrary, her deliberations were of a trivial subject, even ludicrous in any other estimation than her own.

Sol was small, she argued within herself, the jug was large and sticky. He might be tempted to lighten it, for Sol had saccharine predilections, and the helpless jug was at his mercy. Sol had scant judgment and one suit of clothes available; the other, sopping wet from the wash, now swayed in the process of drying on an elder-bush in the dooryard. Should his integrity succumb, and the jug tilt too far, the stream of sorghum might inundate his raiment, and the catastrophe would place him beyond the pale of polite society. The seclusion of bed would be the only place for Sol till such time as the elder-bush should bear the fruit of dry clothes.

"Poor Sol!" she exclaimed, her prophetic sympathy bridging the chasm between possibility and accomplished fact. "I'll fetch the jug myself. I'll take the short cut an' head him."

Thus she set her feet in the path of her future. It led her into dense, tangled woods, clambering over outcropping ledges and boulders. By the flare of the west she guided her progress straight to the east till she reached the banks of Headlong Creek on its tumultuous course down the mountain-side. In her hasty enterprise she had not counted on crossing it, but Meddlesome rarely turned back. She was strong and active, and after a moment's hesitation, she was springing from one to another of the great, half-submerged boulders amidst the whirl of the transparent crystal-brown water, with its fleck and fringe of white foam. More than once, to evade the dizzying effect of the sinuous motion and the continuous roar, she stood still in midstream and gazed upward or at the opposite bank. The woods were dense on the slope. All in red and yellow and variant russet and brown tints, the canopy of the forest foliage was impenetrable. The great, dark boles of oak and gum and spruce contrasted sharply with the white and greenish-gray trunks of beeches and sycamore and poplar, and, thus breaking the monotony, gave long, almost illimitable avenues of sylvan vistas. She noted amidst a growth of willows on the opposite bank, at the water's-edge, a spring, a circular, rockbound reservoir; in the marshy margin she could see the imprints of the cleft hoofs of deer, and thence ran the indefinite trail known as a deer-path. The dense covert along the steep slope was a famous "deer-stand," and there many a fine buck had been killed. All at once she was reminded of the storied tree hard by, the tragedy of which she had often bewept.

There it stood, dead itself, weird, phantasmal, as befitted the housing of so drear a fate. Its branches now bore no leaves. The lightnings of a last-year's storm had scorched out its vital force and riven the fibre of the wood. Here and there, too, the tooth of decay had gnawed fissures that the bark had not earlier known; and from one of these—she thought herself in a dream— a ghastly, white face looked out suddenly, and as suddenly vanished!

Her heart gave one wild plunge, then it

seemed to cease to beat. She wondered afterward that she did not collapse, and sink into the plunging rapids to drown, beaten and bruised against the rocks. It was a muscular instinct that sustained her rather than a conscious impulse of self-preservation. Motionless, horrified, amazed, she could only gaze at the empty fissure of the tree on the slope. She could not then discriminate the wild, spectral imaginations that assailed her untutored mind. She could not remember these fantasies later. It was a relief so great that the anguish of the physical reaction was scarcely less poignant than the original shock when she realized that this face was not the grisly skeleton lineaments that had looked out thence heretofore, but was clothed with flesh, though gaunt, pallid, furtive. Once more, as she gazed, it appeared in a mere glimpse at the fissure, and in that instant a glance was interchanged. The next moment a hand appeared,—beckoning her to approach.

It was a gruesome mandate. She had scant choice. She did not doubt that this was the fugitive, the "wolf's head," and should she turn to flee, he could stop her progress with a pistol-ball, for doubtless he would fancy her alert to disclose the discovery and share in the reward. Perhaps feminine curiosity aided fear; perhaps only her proclivity to find an employ in the management of others influenced her decision; though trembling in every fibre, she crossed the interval of water, and made her way up the slope. But when she reached the fateful tree it was she who spoke first. He cast so ravenous a glance at the basket on her arm that all his story of want and woe was revealed. Starvation had induced his disclosure of his identity.

"It's empty," she said, inverting the basket. She watched him flinch, and asked wonderingly, "Is game skeerce?"

His eyes were at once forlorn and fierce. "Oh, yes, powerful skeerce," he replied with a bitter laugh.

There was an enigma in the rejoinder; she did not stay to read the riddle, but went on to possess the situation, according to her wont. "Ye hev tuk a powerful pore place ter hide," she admonished him. "This tree is a plumb cur'osity. Gran'dad Kettison war tellin' some camp-hunters 'bout'n it jes this evenin'. Like ez not they'll kem ter view it."

His eyes dilated with a sudden accession of terror that seemed always a-smoulder. "Lawd, Lawd, Lawd!" he moaned wretchedly.

Meddlesome was true to her name and tradition. "Ye oughter hev remembered the Lawd 'fore ye done it," she said, with a repellent impulse; then she would have given much to recall the reproach. The man was desperate; his safety lay in her silence. A pistol-shot would secure it, and anger would limber the trigger.

But he did not seem indignant. His eyes, intelligent and feverishly bright, gazed down at her only in obvious dismay and surprise. "Done what?" he asked, and as, prudence prevailing for once, she did not reply, he spoke for her. "The murder, ye mean? Why, gal, I warn't even thar. I knowed nuthin' 'bout it till later. Ez God is my helper and my hope, I warn't even thar."

She stood astounded. "Then why n't ye leave it ter men?"

"I can't *prove* it ag'in' the murderers' oaths. I had been consarned in the moonshinin' that ended in murder, but *I* hed not been nigh the still fer a month,—I war out a-huntin'—when the revenuers made the raid. There war a scrimmage 'twixt the raiders an' the distillers, an' an outsider that hed nuthin' ter do with the Federal law—he war the constable o' the deestrick, an' jes rid with the gang ter see the fun or ter show them the way—he war killed. An' account o' *him*, the State law kem into the game. Them other moonshiners war captured, an' they swore ag'in' me 'bout the shootin' ter save tharselves, but I hearn thar false oaths hev done them no good, they being held as accessory. An' I be so ez I can't prove an alibi—I can't *prove* it, though it's God's truth. But before high heaven"—he lifted his gaunt right hand—"I am innercent, I am innercent."

She could not have said why,—perhaps she realized afterward,—but she believed him absolutely, implicitly. A fervor of sympathy for his plight, of commiseration, surged up in her heart. "I wisht it war so I could gin ye some pervisions," she sighed, "though ye do 'pear toler'ble triflin' ter lack game."

Then the dread secret was told. "Gal,"

—he used the word as a polite form of address, the equivalent of the more sophisticated "lady,"—"ef ye will believe me, all my ammunition is spent. Not a ca'tridge lef', not a dust of powder."

Meddy caught both her hands to her lips to intercept and smother a cry of dismay.

"I snared a rabbit two days ago in a dead-fall. My knife-blade is bruk, but I reckon thar is enough lef' ter split my jugular whenst the eend is kem at last."

The girl suddenly caught her faculties together. "What sorter fool talk is that?" she demanded sternly. "Ye do my bid, ef ye knows what's good fer ye. Git out'n this trap of a tree an' hide 'mongst the crevices of the rocks till seben o'clock ternight. Then kem up ter Gran'dad Kettison's whenst it is cleverly dark an' tap on the glass winder— not on the batten shutter. An' I'll hev ca'tridges an' powder an' ball for ye, an' some victuals ready, too."

But the fugitive, despite his straits, demurred. "I don't want ter git old man Kettison into trouble for lendin' ter me."

" 'T ain't his'n. 'T is my dad's old buckshot ca'tridges an' powder an' ball. They belong ter *me*. The other childern is my half-brothers, bein' my mother war married twice. Ye kin *steal* this gear from me, ef that will make ye feel easier."

"But what will yer gran'dad say ter me?"

"He won't know who ye be; he will jes 'low ye air one o' the boys who air always foolin' away thar time visitin' me an' makin' tallow-dips skeerce." The sudden gleam of mirth on her face was like an illuminating burst of sunshine, and somehow it cast an irradiation into the heart of the fugitive, for, after she was gone out of sight, he pondered upon it.

But the early dusk fell from a lowering sky, and the night came on beclouded and dark. Some turbulent spirit was loosed in the air, and the wind was wild. Great, surging masses of purple vapor came in a mad rout from the dank west and gathered above the massive and looming mountains. The woods bent and tossed and clashed their boughs in the riot of gusts, the sere leaves were flying in clouds, and presently rain began to fall. The steady downpour increased in volume to torrents; then the broad, pervasive flashes of lightning showed, in lieu of myriad lines, an unbroken veil of steely gray swinging from the zenith, the white foam rebounding as the masses of water struck the earth. The camp equipage, tents and wagons succumbed beneath the fury of the tempest, and, indeed, the hunters had much ado to saddle their horses and grope their way along the bridle-path that led to old Kettison's house.

The rude comfort of the interior had a heightened emphasis by reason of the elemental turmoils without. True, the rain beat in a deafening fusillade upon the roof, and the ostentation of the one glass window, a source of special pride to its owner, was at a temporary disadvantage in admitting the fierce and ghastly electric glare, so recurrent as to seem unintermittent. But the more genial illumination of hickory flames, red and yellow, was streaming from the great chimney-place, and before the broad hearth the guests were ensconced, their outstretched boots steaming in the heat. Strings of scarlet peppers, bunches of dried herbs, gourds of varied quaint shapes, hung swaying from the rafters. The old man's gay, senile chirp of welcome was echoed by his wife, a type of comely rustic age, who made much of the fact that, though housebound from "rheumatics," she had reared her dead daughter's "two orphin famblies," the said daughter having married twice, neither man "bein' of a lastin' quality," as she seriously phrased it. Meddy, "the eldest fambly," had been guide, philosopher, and friend to the swarm of youngsters, and even now, in the interests of peace and space and hearing, was seeking to herd them into an adjoining room, when a sudden stentorian hail from without rang through the splashing of the rain from the eaves, the crash of thunder among the "balds" of the mountains, with its lofty echoes, and the sonorous surging of the wind.

"Light a tallow-dip, Meddy," cried old Kettison, excitedly. "An' fetch the candle on the porch so ez we-uns kin view who rides so late in sech a night 'fore we bid 'em ter light an' hitch."

But these were travelers not to be gainsaid—the sheriff of the county and four stout fellows from the town of Colbury, summoned to his aid as a posse, all trooping in as if they owned the little premises. However, the officer permitted himself to unbend a trifle under the influence of a hospitable tender of home-made cherry-bounce, "strong enough to walk from here to Colbury," according to the sheriff's appreciative phrase. He was a portly man, with a rolling, explanatory cant of his burly head and figure toward his interlocutor as he talked. His hair stood up in two tufts above his forehead, one on each side, and he had large, round, grayish eyes and a solemn, pondering expression. To Meddy, staring horror-stricken, he seemed as owlishly wise as he looked while he explained the object of his expedition.

"This district have got a poor reputation with the law, Mr. Kettison. Here is this fellow, Royston McGurny, been about here two years, and a reward for five hundred dollars out for his arrest."

"That's Roy's fault, Sher'ff, not our'n," leered the glib old man. He, too, had had a sip of the stalwart cherry-bounce. "Roy's in no wise sociable."

"It's plumb flying in the face of the law," declared the officer. "If I had a guide, I'd not wait a minute, or if I could recognize the man whenst I viewed him. The constable promised to send a fellow to meet me here, —what's his name?—yes, Smith, Barton Smith,—who will guide us to where he was last glimpsed. I hope to take him alive," he added with an inflection of doubt.

Certainly this was a dreary camp-hunt, with all its distasteful sequelæ. Purcell, who had no more imagination than a promissory note, silently sulked under the officer's intimation that, being able-bodied men, he would expect the hunters also to ride with him. They were not of his county, and doubted their obligation, but they would not refuse to aid the law. Bygrave, however, realized a "story" in the air, and Seymour was interested in the impending developments; for being a close observer, he had perceived that the girl was in the clutch of some tumultuous though covert agitation. Her blood blazed at fever-heat in her cheeks; her eyes were on fire; every muscle was tense; and her brain whirled. To her the crisis was tremendous. This was the result of her unwarranted interference. Who was she, indeed, that she should seek to command the march of events and deploy sequences? Her foolish manœuvering had lured this innocent man to ruin, capture, anguish, and death. No warning could he have; the window was opaque with the corrugations of the rainfall on the streaming panes, and set too high to afford him a glimpse from without. And, oh, how he would despise the traitor that she must needs seem to be! She had not a moment for reflection, for counsel, for action. Already the signal,—he was prompt at the tryst,—the sharp, crystalline vibration of the tap on the glass!

The sheriff rose instantly with that cumbrous agility sometimes characterizing portly men. "There he is now!" he exclaimed.

But Meddy, with a little hysterical cry, had sprung first to the opening door. "Barton Smith!" she exclaimed, with shrill significance. "Hyar is yer guide, Sher'ff, wet ez a drownded rat."

The pale face in the dark aperture of the doorway, as the fire-light flashed on it, grew ghastly white with terror and lean with amazement. For a moment the man seemed petrified. Seymour, vaguely fumbling with his suspicions, began to disintegrate the plot of the play, and to discriminate the powers of the dramatis personæ.

"Now, my man, step lively," said the officer in his big, husky voice. "Do you know this Royston McGurny?"

To be sure, Seymour had no cause for suspicion but his own intuition and the intangible evidence of tone and look all as obvious to the others as to him. But he was at once doubtful and relieved when the haggard wretch at the door, mustering his courage, replied: "Know Royston McGurny? None better. Knowed him all my life."

"Got pretty good horse?"

"Got none at all; expect ter borry Mr. Kettison's."

"I'll go show ye whar the saddle be," exclaimed Meddy, with her wonted officiousness, and glibly picking up the bits of her shattered scheme. Seymour fully expected they would not return from the gloom without, whither they had disappeared, but embrace the immediate chance of escape before the inopportune arrival of the real Barton Smith should balk the possibility. But, no,—and he doubted anew all his suspicions, —in a trice here they both were again, a new courage, a new hope in that pallid, furtive face, and another horse stood saddled among the equine group at the door. Meddlesome was pinning up the brown skirt of her gown, showing a red petticoat that had harmonies with a coarse, red plaid shawl adjusted over her head and shoulders.

"Gran'dad," she observed, never looking up, and speaking with her mouth full of pins, "Barton Smith say he kin set me down at Aunt Drusina's house. Ye know she be ailin', an' sent for me this evenin'; but I hed no way ter go."

The sheriff looked sour enough at this intrusion; but he doubtless imagined that this relative was no distant neighbor, and as he had need of hearty aid and popular support, he offered no protest.

There was a clearing sky without, and the wind was laid. The frenzy of the storm was over, although rain was still falling. The little cavalcade got to horse deliberately enough amid the transparent dun shadows and dim yellow flare of light from open door and window. One of the mounts had burst a girth, and a strap must be procured from the plow-gear in the shed. Another, a steed of some spirit, reared and plunged at the lights, and could not be induced to cross the

WOLF'S HEAD

illuminated bar thrown athwart the yard from the open door. The official impatience of the delay was expressed in irritable comments and muttered oaths; but throughout the interval the guide, with his pallid, strained face, sat motionless in his saddle, his rifle across its pommel, an apt presentment of indifference, while, perched behind him, Meddy was continually busy in readjusting her skirts or shawl or a small bundle that presumably contained her rustic finery, but which, to a close approach, would have disclosed the sulphurous odor of gunpowder.

When the cluster of horsemen was fairly on the march, however, she sat quite still, and more than once Seymour noted that, with her face close to the shoulder of the guide, she was whispering in his ear. What was their game? he marvelled, having once projected the idea that this late comer was, himself, the "wolf's head" whom they were to chase down for a rich reward, incongruously hunting amidst his own hue and cry. Or, Seymour again doubted, had he merely constructed a figment of a scheme from his own imaginings and these attenuations of suggestion? For there seemed, after all, scant communication between the two, and this was even less when the moon was unveiled, the shifting shimmer of the clouds falling away from the great sphere of pearl, gemming the night with an incomparable splendor. It had grown almost as light as day, and the sheriff ordered the pace quickened. Along a definite cattle-trail they went at first, but presently they were following through bosky recesses a deer-path, winding sinuously at will on the way to water. The thinning foliage let in the fair, ethereal light, and all the sylvan aisles stood in sheeny silver illumination. The drops of moisture glittered jewel-wise on the dark boughs of fir and pine, and one could even discriminate the red glow of sour-wood and the golden flare of hickory, so well were the chromatic harmonies asserted in this refined and refulgent glamour.

"Barton Smith!" called the sheriff, suddenly from the rear of the party. There was no answer, and Seymour felt his prophetic blood run cold. His conscience began to stir. Had he, indeed, no foundation for his suspicion?

"Smith! *Smith*" cried the irascible officer. "Hey, there! Is the man deaf?"

"Not deef, edzac'ly," Meddlesome's voice sounded reproachfully; "jes a leetle hard o' hearin'." She had administered a warning nudge.

"Hey? What ye want?" said the "Wolf's Head," suddenly checking his horse.

"Have you any idea of where you are going, or how far?" demanded the officer, sternly.

"Just acrost the gorge," the guide answered easily.

"I heard he had been glimpsed in a hollow tree. That word was telephoned from the cross-roads to town. It was the tree the skeleton was in."

"That tree? It's away back yander," observed one of the posse, reluctant and disaffected.

"Oh, he has quit that tree; he is bound for up the gorge now," said the guide.

"Well, I suppose you know, from what I was told," said the sheriff, discontentedly; "but this is a long ja'nt. Ride up! Ride up!"

Onward they fared through the perfumed woods. The wild asters were blooming, and sweet and subtile distillations of the autumnal growths were diffused on the air. The deer are but ill at road-making,— such tangled coverts, such clifty ledges, such wild leaps; for now the path threaded the jagged verge of precipices. The valley, a black abyss above which massive, purplish mountains loomed against a sky of pearly tints, was visibly narrowing. They all knew that presently it would become a mere gorge, a vast indentation in the mountain-side. The weird vistas across the gorge were visible now, craggy steeps, and deep woods filled with moonlight, with that peculiar untranslated intendment which differentiates its luminosity in the wilderness from the lunar glamour of cultivated scenes—something weird, melancholy, eloquent of a meaning addressed to the soul, but which the senses cannot entertain or words express.

With a sudden halt, the guide dismounted. The girl still sat on the saddle-blanket, and the horse bowed his head and pawed. The posse were gazing dubiously, reluctantly, at a foot-bridge across a deep abyss. It was only a log, the upper side hewn, with a shaking hand-rail held by slight standards.

"Have we got to cross this?" asked the

officer, still in the saddle and gazing downward.

"Ef ye foller me," said the guide, indifferently.

But he was ahead of his orders. He visibly braced his nerves for the effort, and holding his rifle as a balancing-pole, he sped along the light span with a tread as deft as a fox or a wolf. In a moment he had gained the farther side.

They scarcely knew how it happened. So unexpected was the event that, though it occurred before their eyes, they did not seem to see it. They remembered, rather than perceived, that he stooped suddenly; with one single great effort of muscular force he dislodged the end of the log, heaved it up in the air, strongly flung it aside, whence it went crashing down into the black depths below, its own weight, as it fell, sufficing to wrench out the other end, carrying with it a mass of earth and rock from the verge of the precipice.

The horses sprang back snorting and frightened; the officer's, being a fine animal in prime condition, tried to bolt. Before he had him well in hand again, the man on the opposite brink had vanished. The sheriff's suspicions were barely astir when a hallooing voice in the rear made itself heard, and a horseman, breathless with haste, his steed flecked with foam, rode up, indignant, flushed, and eager.

"Whyn't ye wait for me, Sher'ff? Ye air all on the wrong track," he cried. "Royston McGurny be hid in the skellington's tree. I glimpsed him thar myself, an' gin information."

The sheriff gazed down with averse and suspicious eyes. "What's all this?" he said sternly. "Give an account of yourself."

"Me?" exclaimed the man in amazement. "Why, I'm Barton Smith, yer guide, that's who. An' I'm good for five hundred dollars' reward."

But the sheriff called off the pursuit for the time, as he had no means of replacing the bridge or of crossing the chasm.

Meddlesome's share in the escape was not detected, and for a while she had no incentive to the foolhardiness of boasting. But her prudence diminished when the reward for the apprehension of Royston McGurny was suddenly withdrawn. The con-

WOLF'S HEAD

fession of one of the distillers, dying of tuberculosis contracted in prison, who had himself fired the fatal shot, had established the alibi that McGurny claimed, and served to relieve him of all suspicion.

He eventually became a "herder" of cattle on the bald of the mountain and a farmer in a small way, and in these placid pursuits he found a contented existence. But, occasionally, a crony of his olden time would contrast the profits of this tame industry at a disadvantage with the quick and large returns of the "wild cat," when he would "confess and avoid."

"That's true, that's all true; but a man can't holp it no ways in the world whenst he hev got a wife that is so out-an'-out meddlesome that she won't let him run ag'in' the law, nohow he kin fix it."

HIS UNQUIET GHOST

The moon was high in the sky. The wind was laid. So silent was the vast stretch of mountain wilderness, aglint with the dew, that the tinkle of a rill far below in the black abyss seemed less a sound than an evidence of the pervasive quietude, since so slight a thing, so distant, could compass so keen a vibration. For an hour or more the three men who lurked in the shadow of a crag in the narrow mountain-pass, heard nothing else. When at last they caught the dull reverberation of a slow wheel and the occasional metallic clank of a tire against a stone, the vehicle was fully three miles distant by the winding road in the valley. Time lagged. Only by imperceptible degrees the sound of deliberate approach grew louder on the air as the interval of space lessened. At length, above their ambush at the summit of the mountain's brow the heads of horses came into view, distinct in the moonlight between the fibrous pines and the vast expanse of the sky above the valley. Even then there was renewed delay. The driver of the wagon paused to rest the team.

HIS UNQUIET GHOST

The three lurking men did not move; they scarcely ventured to breathe. Only when there was no retrograde possible, no chance of escape, when the vehicle was fairly on the steep declivity of the road, the precipice sheer on one side, the wall of the ridge rising perpendicularly on the other, did two of them, both revenue-raiders disguised as mountaineers, step forth from the shadow. The other, the informer, a genuine mountaineer, still skulked motionless in the darkness. The "revenuers," ascending the road, maintained a slow, lunging gait, as if they had toiled from far.

Their abrupt appearance had the effect of a galvanic shock to the man handling the reins, a stalwart, rubicund fellow, who visibly paled. He drew up so suddenly as almost to throw the horses from their feet.

"G'evenin'," ventured Browdie, the elder of the raiders, in a husky voice affecting an untutored accent. He had some special ability as a mimic, and, being familiar with the dialect and manners of the people, this gift greatly facilitated the rustic impersonation he had essayed. "Ye're haulin' late," he added, for the hour was close to midnight.

"Yes, stranger; haulin' late, from Eskaqua—a needcessity."

"What's yer cargo?" asked Browdie, seeming only ordinarily inquisitive.

A sepulchral cadence was in the driver's voice, and the disguised raiders noted that the three other men on the wagon had preserved, throughout, a solemn silence. "What we-uns mus' all be one day, stranger—a corpus."

Browdie was stultified for a moment. Then, sustaining his assumed character, he said: "I hope it be nobody I know. I be fairly well acquainted in Eskaqua, though I hail from down in Lonesome Cove. Who be dead?"

There was palpably a moment's hesitation before the spokesman replied: "Watt Wyatt; died day 'fore yestiddy."

At the words, one of the silent men in the wagon turned his face suddenly, with such obvious amazement depicted upon it that it arrested the attention of the "revenuers." This face was so individual that it was not likely to be easily mistaken or forgotten. A wild, breezy look it had, and a tricksy, incorporeal expression that might well befit some fantastic, fabled thing of the woods. It was full of fine script of elusive meanings, not registered in the lineaments of the prosaic man of the day, though perchance of scant utility, not worth interpretation. His full gray eyes were touched to glancing brilliancy by a moonbeam; his long, fibrously floating brown hair was thrown backward; his receding chin was peculiarly delicate; and though his well-knit frame bespoke a hardy vigor, his pale cheek was soft and thin. All the rustic grotesquery of garb and posture was cancelled by the deep shadow of a bough, and his delicate face showed isolated in the moonlight.

Browdie silently pondered his vague suspicions for a moment. "Whar did he die at?" he then demanded at a venture.

"At his daddy's house, fur sure. Whar else?" responded the driver. "I hev got what's lef' of him hyar in the coffin-box. We expected ter make it ter Shiloh buryin'-ground 'fore dark; but the road is middlin' heavy, an' 'bout five mile' back Ben cast a shoe. The funeral warn't over much 'fore noon."

"Whyn't they bury him in Eskaqua, whar he died?" persisted Browdie.

"Waal, they planned ter bury him alongside his mother an' gran'dad, what used ter live in Tanglefoot Cove. But we air wastin' time hyar, an' we hev got none ter spare. Gee, Ben! Git up, John!"

The wagon gave a lurch; the horses, holding back in bracing attitudes far from the pole, went teetering down the steep slant, the locked wheel dragging heavily; the four men sat silent, two in slouching postures at the head of the coffin; the third, with the driver, was at its foot. It seemed drearily suggestive, the last journey of this humble mortality, in all the splendid environment of the mountains, under the vast expansions of the aloof skies, in the mystic light of the unnoting moon.

"Is this bona-fide?" asked Browdie, with a questioning glance at the informer, who had at length crept forth.

"I dunno," sullenly responded the mountaineer. He had acquainted the two officers, who were of a posse of revenue-raiders hovering in the vicinity, with the mysterious circumstance that a freighted wagon now and then made a midnight transit across these lonely ranges. He himself had heard only occasionally in a wakeful hour the roll of heavy wheels, but he interpreted this as the secret transportation of brush whisky from the still to its market. He had thought to fix the transgression on an old enemy of his own, long suspected of moonshining; but he was acquainted with none of the youngsters on the wagon, at whom he had peered cautiously from behind the rocks. His actuating motive in giving information to the emissaries of the government had been the rancor of an old feud, and his detection meant certain death. He had not expected the revenue-raiders to be outnumbered by the supposed moonshiners, and he would not fight in the open. He had no sentiment of fealty to the law, and the officers glanced at each other in uncertainty.

"This evidently is not the wagon in question," said Browdie, disappointed.

"I'll follow them a bit," volunteered Ronan, the younger and the more active of the two officers. "Seems to me they'll bear watching."

Indeed, as the melancholy cortège fared down and down the steep road, dwindling in the sheeny distance, the covert and half-suppressed laughter of the sepulchral escort was of so keen a relish that it was well that the scraping of the locked wheel aided the distance to mask the incongruous sound.

"What ailed you-uns ter name *me* as the corpus, 'Gene Barker?" demanded Walter Wyatt, when he had regained the capacity of coherent speech.

"Oh, I hed ter do suddint murder on somebody," declared the driver, all bluff and reassured and red-faced again, "an' I couldn't think quick of nobody else. Besides, I helt a grudge ag'in' you fer not stuffin' mo' straw 'twixt them jimmyjohns in the coffin-box."

"That's a fac'. Ye air too triflin' ter be let ter live, Watt," cried one of their comrades. "I hearn them jugs clash tergether in the coffin-box when 'Gene checked the team up suddint, I tell you. An' them men sure 'peared ter me powerful suspectin'."

"*I* hearn the clash of them jimmyjohns," chimed in the driver. "I really thunk my hour war come. Some informer must hev set them men ter spyin' round fer moonshine."

"Oh, surely nobody wouldn't dare," urged one of the group, uneasily; for the identity of an informer was masked in secrecy, and his fate, when discovered, was often gruesome.

"They couldn't hev noticed the clash of them jimmyjohns, nohow," declared the negligent Watt, nonchalantly. "But namin' *me* fur the dead one! Supposin' they air revenuers fur true, an' hed somebody along, hid out in the bresh, ez war acquainted with me by sight——"

"Then they'd hev been skeered out'n thar boots, that's all," interrupted the self-sufficient 'Gene. "They would hev 'lowed they hed viewed yer brazen ghost, bold ez brass, standin' at the head of yer own coffin-box."

"Or mebbe they mought hev recognized the Wyatt favor, ef they warn't acquainted with *me*," persisted Watt, with his unique sense of injury.

Eugene Barker defended the temerity of his inspiration. "They would hev jes thought ye war kin ter the deceased, an' attendin' him ter his long home."

" 'Gene don't keer much fur ye ter be alive nohow, Watt Wyatt," one of the others suggested tactlessly, " 'count o' Minta Elladine Riggs."

HIS UNQUIET GHOST

Eugene Barker's off-hand phrase was incongruous with his sudden gravity and his evident rancor as he declared: "*I* ain't carin' fur sech ez Watt Wyatt. An' they *do* say in the cove that Minta Elladine Riggs hev gin him the mitten, anyhow, on account of his gamesome ways, playin' kyerds, a-bettin' his money, drinkin' apple-jack, an' sech.''

The newly constituted ghost roused himself with great vitality as if to retort floutingly; but as he turned, his jaw suddenly fell; his eyes widened with a ghastly distension. With an unsteady arm extended he pointed silently. Distinctly outlined on the lid of the coffin was the simulacrum of the figure of a man.

One of his comrades, seated on the tail-board of the wagon, had discerned a significance in the abrupt silence. As he turned, he, too, caught a fleeting glimpse of that weird image on the coffin-lid. But he was of a more mundane pulse. The apparition roused in him only a wonder whence could come this shadow in the midst of the moon-flooded road. He lifted his eyes to the verge of the bluff above, and there he descried an indistinct human form, which sud-

HIS UNQUIET GHOST

denly disappeared as he looked, and at that moment the simulacrum vanished from the lid of the box.

The mystery was of instant elucidation. They were suspected, followed. The number of their pursuers of course they could not divine, but at least one of the revenue-officers had trailed the wagon between the precipice and the great wall of the ascent on the right, which had gradually dwindled to a diminished height. Deep gullies were here and there washed out by recent rains, and one of these indentations might have afforded an active man access to the summit. Thus the pursuer had evidently kept abreast of them, speeding along in great leaps through the lush growth of huckleberry bushes, wild grasses, pawpaw thickets, silvered by the moon, all fringing the great forests that had given way on the shelving verge of the steeps where the road ran. Had he overheard their unguarded, significant words? Who could divine, so silent were the windless mountains, so deep a-dream the darksome woods, so spellbound the mute and mystic moonlight?

The group maintained a cautious reticence now, each revolving the problematic disclosure of their secret, each canvassing the question whether the pursuer himself was aware of his betrayal of his stealthy proximity. Not till they had reached the ford of the river did they venture on a low-toned colloquy. The driver paused in midstream and stepped out on the pole between the horses to let down the check-reins, as the team manifested an inclination to drink in transit; and thence, as he stood thus perched, he gazed to and fro, the stretch of dark and lustrous ripples baffling all approach within ear-shot, the watering of the horses justifying the pause and cloaking its significance to any distant observer.

But the interval was indeed limited; the mental processes of such men are devoid of complexity, and their decisions prompt. They advanced few alternatives; their prime object was to be swiftly rid of the coffin and its inculpating contents, and with the "revenuer" so hard on their heels this might seem a troublous problem enough.

"Put it whar a coffin b'longs—in the churchyard," said Wyatt; for at a considerable distance beyond the rise of the opposite

HIS UNQUIET GHOST

bank could be seen a barren clearing in which stood a gaunt, bare, little white frame building that served all the country-side for its infrequent religious services.

"We couldn't dig a grave before that spy—ef he be a revenuer sure enough—could overhaul us," Eugene Barker objected.

"We could turn the yearth right smart, though," persisted Wyatt, for pickax and shovel had been brought in the wagon for the sake of an aspect of verisimilitude and to mask their true intent.

Eugene Barker acceded to this view. "That's the dinctum—dig a few jes fer a blind. We kin slip the coffin-box under the church-house 'fore he gits in sight,—he'll be feared ter follow too close,—an' leave it thar till the other boys kin wagon it ter the cross-roads' store ter-morrer night."

The horses, hitherto held to the sober gait of funeral travel, were now put to a speedy trot, unmindful of whatever impression of flight the pace might give to the revenue-raider in pursuit. The men were soon engrossed in their deceptive enterprise in the churchyard, plying pickax and shovel for dear life; now and again they paused to listen vainly for the sound of stealthy approach. They knew that there was the most precarious and primitive of foot-bridges across the deep stream, to traverse which would cost an unaccustomed wayfarer both time and pains; thus the interval was considerable before the resonance of rapid footfalls gave token that their pursuer had found himself obliged to sprint smartly along the country road to keep any hope of ever again viewing the wagon which the intervening water-course had withdrawn from his sight. That this hope had grown tenuous was evident in his relinquishment of his former caution, for when they again caught a glimpse of him he was forging along in the middle of the road without any effort at concealment. But as the wagon appeared in the perspective, stationary, hitched to the hedge of the graveyard, he recurred to his previous methods. The four men still within the inclosure, now busied in shovelling the earth back again into the excavation they had so swiftly made, covertly watched him as he skulked into the shadow of the wayside. The little "church-house," with all its windows whitely aglare in the moonlight, reflected the

HIS UNQUIET GHOST

pervasive sheen, and silent, spectral, remote, it seemed as if it might well harbor at times its ghastly neighbors from the quiet cemetery without, dimly ranging themselves once more in the shadowy ranks of its pews or grimly stalking down the drear and deserted aisles. The fact that the rising ground toward the rear of the building necessitated a series of steps at the entrance, enabled the officer to mask behind this tall flight his crouching approach, and thus he ensconced himself in the angle between the wall and the steps, and looked forth in fancied security.

The shadows multiplied the tale of the dead that the head-boards kept, each similitude askew in the moonlight on the turf below the slanting monument. To judge by the motions of the men engaged in the burial and the mocking antics of their silhouettes on the ground, it must have been obvious to the spectator that they were already filling in the earth. The interment may have seemed to him suspiciously swift, but the possibility was obvious that the grave might have been previously dug in anticipation of their arrival. It was plain that he was altogether unprepared for the event when they came slouching forth to the wagon, and the stalwart and red-faced driver, with no manifestation of surprise, hailed him as he still crouched in his lurking-place. "Hello, stranger! Warn't that you-uns runnin' arter the wagon a piece back yonder jes a while ago?"

The officer rose to his feet, with an intent look both dismayed and embarrassed. He did not venture on speech; he merely acceded with a nod.

"Ye want a lift, I reckon."

The stranger was hampered by the incongruity between his rustic garb, common to the coves, and his cultivated intonation; for, unlike his comrade Browdie, he had no mimetic faculties whatever. Nevertheless, he was now constrained to "face the music."

"I didn't want to interrupt you," he said, seeking such excuse as due consideration for the circumstances might afford; "but I'd like to ask where I could get lodging for the night."

"What's yer name?" demanded Barker, unceremoniously.

"Francis Ronan," the raider replied, with more assurance. Then he added, by way of explaining his necessity, "I'm a stranger hereabouts."

"Ye air so," assented the sarcastic 'Gene. "Ye ain't even acquainted with yer own clothes. Ye be a town man."

"Well, I'm not the first man who has had to hide out," Ronan parried, seeking to justify his obvious disguise.

"Shot somebody?" asked 'Gene, with an apparent accession of interest.

"It's best for me not to tell."

"So be." 'Gene acquiesced easily. "Waal, ef ye kin put up with sech accommodations ez our'n, I'll take ye home with me."

Ronan stood aghast. But there was no door of retreat open. He was alone and helpless. He could not conceal the fact that the turn affairs had taken was equally unexpected and terrifying to him, and the moonshiners, keenly watchful, were correspondingly elated to discern that he had surely no reinforcements within reach to nerve him to resistance or to menace their liberty. He had evidently followed them too far, too recklessly; perhaps without the consent and against the counsel of his comrades, perhaps even without their knowledge of his movements and intention.

Now and again as the wagon jogged on and on toward their distant haven, the moonlight gradually dulling to dawn, Wyatt gave the stranger a wondering, covert glance, vaguely, shrinkingly curious as to the sentiments of a man vacillating between the suspicion of capture and the recognition of a simple hospitality without significance or danger. The man's face appealed to him, young, alert, intelligent, earnest, and the anguish of doubt and anxiety it expressed went to his heart. In the experience of his sylvan life as a hunter Wyatt's peculiar and subtle temperament evolved certain fine-spun distinctions which were unique; a trapped thing had a special appeal to his commiseration that a creature ruthlessly slaughtered in the open was not privileged to claim. He did not accurately and in words discriminate the differences, but he felt that the captive had sounded all the gamut of hope and despair, shared the gradations of an appreciated sorrow that makes all souls akin and that even lifts the beast to the plane of brotherhood, the bond of emotional woe. He had

HIS UNQUIET GHOST

often with no other or better reason liberated the trophy of his snare, calling after the amazed and franticly fleeing creature, "Bye-bye, Buddy!" with peals of his whimsical, joyous laughter.

He was experiencing now a similar sequence of sentiments in noting the wild-eyed eagerness with which the captured raider took obvious heed of every minor point of worthiness that might mask the true character of his entertainers. But, indeed, these deceptive hopes might have been easily maintained by one not so desirous of reassurance when, in the darkest hour before the dawn, they reached a large log-cabin sequestered in dense woods, and he found himself an inmate of a simple, typical mountain household. It held an exceedingly venerable grandfather, wielding his infirmities as a rod of iron; a father and mother, hearty, hospitable, subservient to the aged tyrant, but keeping in filial check a family of sons and daughters-in-law, with an underfoot delegation of grandchildren, who seemed to spend their time in a bewildering manœuvre of dashing out at one door to dash in at another. A tumultuous rain had set in shortly after dawn, with lightning and wind,—"the tail of a harricane," as the host called it,—and a terrible bird the actual storm must have been to have a tail of such dimensions. There was no getting forth, no living creature of free will "took water" in this elemental crisis. The numerous dogs crowded the children away from the hearth, and the hens strolled about the large living-room, clucking to scurrying broods. Even one of the horses tramped up on the porch and looked in ever and anon, solicitous of human company.

"I brung Ben up by hand, like a bottle-fed baby," the hostess apologized, "an' he ain't never f'und out fur sure that he ain't folks."

There seemed no possible intimation of moonshine in this entourage, and the coffin filled with jugs, a-wagoning from some distillers' den in the range to the cross-roads' store, might well have been accounted only the vain phantasm of an overtired brain surcharged with the vexed problems of the revenue service. The disguised revenue-raider was literally overcome with drowsiness, the result of his exertions and his vigils, and observing this, his host gave him one of the big feather beds under the low slant of the eaves in the roof-room, where the other men, who had been out all night, also slept the greater portion of the day. In fact, it was dark when Wyatt wakened, and, leaving the rest still torpid with slumber and fatigue, descended to the large main room of the cabin.

The callow members of the household had retired to rest, but the elders of the band of moonshiners were up and still actively astir, and Wyatt experienced a prescient vicarious qualm to note their lack of heed or secrecy—the noisy shifting of heavy weights (barrels, kegs, bags of apples, and peaches for pomace), the loud voices and unguarded words. When a door in the floor was lifted, the whiff of chill, subterranean air that pervaded the whole house was heavily freighted with spirituous odors, and gave token to the meanest intelligence, to the most unobservant inmate, that the still was operated in a cellar, peculiarly immune to suspicion, for a cellar is never an adjunct to the ordinary mountain cabin. Thus the infraction of the revenue law went on securely and continuously beneath the placid, simple, domestic life, with its reverent care for the very aged and its tender nurture of the very young.

It was significant, indeed, that the industry should not be pretermitted, however, when a stranger was within the gates. The reason to Wyatt, familiar with the moonshiners' methods and habits of thought, was only too plain. They intended that the "revenuer" should never go forth to tell the tale. His comrades had evidently failed to follow his trail, either losing it in the wilderness or from ignorance of his intention. He had put himself hopelessly into the power of these desperate men, whom his escape or liberation would menace with incarceration for a long term as Federal prisoners in distant penitentiaries, if, indeed, they were not already answerable to the law for some worse crime than illicit distilling. His murder would be the extreme of brutal craft, so devised as to seem an accident, against the possibility of future investigation.

The reflection turned Wyatt deathly cold, he who could not bear unmoved the plea of a wild thing's eye. He sturdily sought to pull himself together. It was none of his decree; it was none of his deed, he argued. The older moonshiners, who managed all the details of the enterprise, would direct the event with absolute authority and the immutability of fate. But whatever should be done, he revolted from any knowledge of it, as from any share in the act. He had risen to leave the place, all strange of aspect now, metamorphosed,—various disorderly details of the prohibited industry ever and anon surging up from the still-room below,— when a hoarse voice took cognizance of his intention with a remonstrance.

"Why, Watt Wyatt, *ye* can't go out in the cove. Ye air dead! Ye will let that t'other revenue-raider ye seen into the secret o' the bresh whisky in our wagon ef ye air viewed about whenst 'Gene hev spread the report that ye air dead. Wait till them raiders hev cleared out of the kentry."

The effort at detention, to interfere with his liberty, added redoubled impetus to Wyatt's desire to be gone. He suddenly devised a cogent necessity. "I be feared my dad mought hear that fool tale. I ain't much loss, but dad would feel it."

"Oh, I sent Jack thar ter tell him better whenst he drove ter mill ter-day ter git the meal fer the mash. Jack made yer dad onderstand 'bout yer sudden demise."

"Oh, yeh," interposed the glib Jack; "an' he said ez *he* couldn't abide sech jokes."

"Shucks!" cried the filial Wyatt. "Dad war full fresky himself in his young days; I hev hearn his old frien's say so."

"I tried ter slick things over," said the diplomatic Jack. "I 'lowed young folks war giddy by nature. I 'lowed 't war jes a flash o' fun. An' he say: 'Flash o' fun be consarned! My son is more like a flash o' lightning; ez suddint an' mischeevious an' totally ondesirable.' "

The reproach obviously struck home, for Wyatt maintained a disconsolate silence for a time. At length, apparently goaded by his thoughts to attempt a defense, he remonstrated:

"Nobody ever war dead less of his own free will. I never elected ter be a harnt. 'Gene Barker hed no right ter nominate *me* fer the dear departed, nohow."

One of the uncouth younger fellows, his shoulders laden with a sack of meal, paused on his way from the porch to the trap-door to look up from beneath his burden with a sly grin as he said, " 'Gene war wishin' it war true, that's why."

" 'Count o' Minta Elladine Riggs," gaily chimed in another.

"But 'Gene needn't gredge Watt foothold on this yearth fer sech; *she* ain't keerin' whether Watt lives or dies," another contributed to the rough, rallying fun.

But Wyatt was of sensitive fibre. He had flushed angrily; his eyes were alight; a bitter retort was trembling on his lips when one of the elder Barkers, discriminating the elements of an uncontrollable fracas, seized on the alternative.

"Could you-uns *sure* be back hyar by daybreak, Watt?" he asked, fixing the young fellow with a stern eye.

"No 'spectable ghost roams around arter sun-up," cried Wyatt, fairly jovial at the prospect of liberation.

"Ye mus' be heedful not ter be viewed," the senior admonished him.

"I be goin' ter slip about keerful like a reg'lar, stiddy-goin' harnt, an' eavesdrop a bit. It's worth livin' a hard life ter view how a feller's friends will take his demise."

HIS UNQUIET GHOST

"I reckon ye kin make out ter meet the wagin kemin' back from the cross-roads' store. It went out this evenin' with that coffin full of jugs that ye lef' las' night under the church-house, whenst 'Gene seen you-uns war suspicioned. They will hev time ter git ter the cross-roads with the whisky on' back little arter midnight, special' ez we-uns hev got the raider that spied out the job hyar fast by the leg."

The mere mention of the young prisoner rendered Wyatt the more eager to be gone, to be out of sight and sound. But he had no agency in the disaster, he urged against some inward clamor of protest; the catastrophe was the logical result of the foolhardiness of the officer in following these desperate men with no backing, with no power to apprehend or hold, relying on his flimsy disguise, and risking delivering himself into their hands, fettered as he was with the knowledge of his discovery of their secret.

"It's nothin' ter *me,* nohow," Wyatt was continually repeating to himself, though when he sprang through the door he could scarcely draw his breath because of some mysterious, invisible clutch at his throat.

HIS UNQUIET GHOST

He sought to ascribe this symptom to the density of the pervasive fog without, that impenetrably cloaked all the world; one might wonder how a man could find his way through the opaque white vapor. It was, however, an accustomed medium to the young mountaineer, and his feet, too, had something of that unclassified muscular instinct, apart from reason, which guides in an oft-trodden path. Once he came to a halt, from no uncertainty of locality, but to gaze apprehensively through the blank, white mists over a shuddering shoulder. "I wonder ef thar be any other harnts aloose ter-night, a-boguing through the fog an' the moon," he speculated. Presently he went on again, shaking his head sagely. "I ain't wantin' ter collogue with sech," he averred cautiously.

Occasionally the moonlight fell in expansive splendor through a rift in the white vapor; amidst the silver glintings a vague, illusory panorama of promontory and island, bay and inlet, far ripplings of gleaming deeps, was presented like some magic reminiscence, some ethereal replica of the past, the simulacrum of the seas of these ancient coves, long since ebbed away and vanished.

HIS UNQUIET GHOST

The sailing moon visibly rocked, as the pulsing tides of the cloud-ocean rose and fell, and ever and anon this supernal craft was whelmed in its surgings, and once more came majestically into view, freighted with fancies and heading for the haven of the purple western shores.

In one of these clearances of the mists a light of an alien type caught the eye of the wandering spectre—a light, red, mundane, of prosaic suggestion. It filtered through the crevice of a small batten shutter.

The ghost paused, his head speculatively askew. "Who sits so late at the forge?" he marvelled, for he was now near the base of the mountain, and he recognized the low, dark building looming through the mists, its roof aslant, its chimney cold, the big doors closed, the shutter fast. As he neared the place a sudden shrill guffaw smote the air, followed by a deep, gruff tone of disconcerted remonstrance. Certain cabalistic words made the matter plain.

"High, Low, Jack, *and* game! Fork! Fork!" Once more there arose a high falsetto shriek of jubilant laughter.

Walter Wyatt crept noiselessly down the

HIS UNQUIET GHOST

steep slant toward the shutter. He had no sense of intrusion, for he was often one of the merry blades wont to congregate at the forge at night and take a hand at cards, despite the adverse sentiment of the cove and the vigilance of the constable of the district, bent on enforcing the laws prohibiting gaming. As Wyatt stood at the crevice of the shutter the whole interior was distinct before him—the disabled wagon-wheels against the walls, the horse-shoes on a rod across the window, the great hood of the forge, the silent bellows, with its long, motionless handle. A kerosene lamp, perched on the elevated hearth of the forge, illumined the group of wild young mountaineers clustered about a barrel on the head of which the cards were dealt. There were no chairs; one of the gamesters sat on a keg of nails; another on an inverted splint basket; two on a rude bench that was wont to be placed outside the door for the accommodation of customers waiting for a horse to be shod or a plow to be laid. An onlooker, not yet so proficient as to attain his ambition of admission to the play, had mounted the anvil, and from this coign of vantage beheld all the outspread

HIS UNQUIET GHOST

landscape of the "hands." More than once his indiscreet, inadvertent betrayal of some incident of his survey of the cards menaced him with a broken head. More innocuous to the interests of the play was a wight humbly ensconced on the shoeing-stool, which barely brought his head to the level of the board; but as he was densely ignorant of the game, he took no disadvantage from his lowly posture. His head was red, and as it moved erratically about in the gloom, Watt Wyatt thought for a moment that it was the smith's red setter. He grinned as he resolved that some day he would tell the fellow this as a pleasing gibe; but the thought was arrested by the sound of his own name.

"Waal, sir," said the dealer, pausing in shuffling the cards, "I s'pose ye hev all hearn 'bout Walter Wyatt's takin' off."

"An' none too soon, sartain." A sour visage was glimpsed beneath the wide brim of the speaker's hat.

"Waal," drawled the semblance of the setter from deep in the clare-obscure, "Watt war jes a fool from lack o' sense."

"That kind o' fool can't be cured," said another of the players. Then he sharply adjured the dealer. "Look out what ye be doin'! Ye hev gimme *two* kyerds."

" 'Gene Barker will git ter marry Minta Elladine Riggs now, I reckon," suggested the man on the anvil.

"An' I'll dance at the weddin' with right good will an' a nimble toe," declared the dealer, vivaciously. "I'll be glad ter see that couple settled. That gal couldn't make up her mind ter let Walter Wyatt go, an' yit no woman in her senses would hev been willin' ter marry him. He war ez onresponsible ez—ez—fox-fire."

"An' ez onstiddy ez a harricane," commented another.

"An' no more account than a mole in the yearth," said a third.

The ghost at the window listened in aghast dismay and became pale in sober truth, for these boon companions he had accounted the best friends he had in the world. They had no word of regret, no simple human pity; even that facile meed of casual praise that he was "powerful pleasant company" was withheld. And for these and such as these he had bartered the esteem of the community at large and his filial duty

HIS UNQUIET GHOST

and obedience; had spurned the claims of good citizenship and placed himself in jeopardy of the law; had forfeited the hand of the woman he loved.

"Minta Elladine Riggs ain't keerin' nohow fer sech ez Watt," said the semblance of the setter, with a knowing nod of his red head. "I war up thar at the mill whenst the news kem ter-day, an' she war thar ter git some seconds. I hev hearn women go off in high-strikes fer a lovyer's death—even Mis' Simton, though hern was jes her husband, an 'a mighty pore one at that. But Minta Elladine jes listened quiet an' composed, an' never said one word."

The batten shutter was trembling in the ghost's hand. In fact, so convulsive was his grasp that it shook the hook from the staple, and the shutter slowly opened as he stood at gaze.

Perhaps it was the motion that attracted the attention of the dealer, perhaps the influx of a current of fresh air. He lifted his casual glance and beheld, distinct in the light from the kerosene lamp and imposed on the white background of the mist, that

HIS UNQUIET GHOST

familiar and individual face, pallid, fixed, strange, with an expression that he had never seen it wear hitherto. One moment of suspended faculties, and he sprang up with a wild cry that filled the little shanty with its shrill terror. The others gazed astounded upon him, then followed the direction of his starting eyes, and echoed his frantic fright. There was a wild scurry toward the door. The overturning of the lamp was imminent, but it still burned calmly on the elevated hearth, while the shoeing-stool capsized in the rush, and the red head of its lowly occupant was lowlier still, rolling on the dirt floor. Even with this disadvantage, however, he was not the hindmost, and reached the exit unhurt. The only specific damage wrought by the panic was to the big barn-like doors of the place. They had been stanchly barred against the possible intrusion of the constable of the district, and the fastenings in so critical an emergency could not be readily loosed. The united weight and impetus of the onset burst the flimsy doors into fragments, and as the party fled in devious directions in the misty moonlight,

HIS UNQUIET GHOST

the calm radiance entered at the wide-spread portal and illuminated the vacant place where late had been so merry a crew.

Walter Wyatt had known the time when the incident would have held an incomparable relish for him. But now he gazed all forlorn into the empty building with a single thought in his mind. "Not one of 'em keered a mite! Nare good word, nare sigh, not even, 'Fare ye well, old mate!' "

His breast heaved, his eyes flashed.

"An' I hev loant money ter Jim, whenst I hed need myself; an' holped George in the mill, when his wrist war sprained, without a cent o' pay; an' took the blame when 'Dolphus war faulted by his dad fur lamin' the horse-critter; an' stood back an' let Pete git the meat whenst we-uns shot fur beef, bein' he hev got a wife an' chil'ren ter feed. All *leetle* favors, but nare *leetle* word."

He had turned from the window and was tramping absently down the road, all unmindful of the skulking methods of the spectral gentry. If he had chanced to be observed, his little farce, that had yet an element of tragedy in its presentation, must soon have reached its close. But the fog

THE UNITED WEIGHT AND IMPETUS OF THE ONSET BURST THE FLIMSY DOORS INTO FRAGMENTS

HIS UNQUIET GHOST

hung about him like a cloak, and when the moon cast aside the vapors, it was in a distant silver sheen illumining the far reaches of the valley. Only when its light summoned forth a brilliant and glancing reflection on a lower level, as if a thousand sabers were unsheathed at a word, he recognized the proximity of the river and came to a sudden halt.

"Whar is this fool goin'?" he demanded angrily of space. "To the graveyard, I declar', ez ef I war a harnt fur true, an' buried sure enough. An' I wish I war. I wish I war."

He realized, after a moment's consideration, that he had been unconsciously actuated by the chance of meeting the wagon, returning by this route from the cross-roads' store. He was tired, disheartened; his spirit was spent; he would be glad of the lift. He reflected, however, that he must needs wait some time, for this was the date of a revival-meeting at the little church, and the distillers' wagon would lag, that its belated night journey might not be subjected to the scrutiny and comment of the church-goers. Indeed, even now Walter Wyatt saw in the distance the glimmer of a lantern, intimating homeward-bound worshipers not yet out of sight.

"The saints kep' it up late ter-night," he commented.

He resolved to wait till the roll of wheels should tell of the return of the moonshiners' empty wagon.

He crossed the river on the little foot-bridge and took his way languidly along the road toward the deserted church. He was close to the hedge that grew thick and rank about the little inclosure when he suddenly heard the sound of lamentation from within. He drew back precipitately, with a sense of sacrilege, but the branches of the unpruned growth had caught in his sleeve, and he sought to disengage the cloth without such rustling stir as might disturb or alarm the mourner, who had evidently lingered here, after the dispersal of the congregation, for a moment's indulgence of grief and despair. He had a glimpse through the shaking boughs and the flickering mist of a woman's figure kneeling on the crude red clods of a new-made grave. A vague, anxious wonder as to the deceased visited him, for in

HIS UNQUIET GHOST

the sparsely settled districts a strong community sense prevails. Suddenly in a choking gust of sobs and burst of tears he recognized his own name in a voice of which every inflection was familiar. For a moment his heart seemed to stand still. His brain whirled with a realization of this unforeseen result of the fantastic story of his death in Eskaqua Cove, which the moonshiners, on the verge of detection and arrest, had circulated in Tanglefoot as a measure of safety. They had fancied that when the truth was developed it would be easy enough to declare the men drunk or mistaken. The "revenuers" by that time would be far away, and the pervasive security, always the sequence of a raid, successful or otherwise, would once more promote the manufacture of the brush whisky. The managers of the moonshining interest had taken measures to guard Wyatt's aged father from this fantasy of woe, but they had not dreamed that the mountain coquette might care. He himself stood appalled that this ghastly fable should delude his heart's beloved, amazed that it should cost her one sigh, one sob. Her racking paroxysms of grief over this gruesome figment of a grave he was humiliated to hear, he was woeful to see. He felt that he was not worth one tear of the floods with which she bewept his name, uttered in every cadence of tender regret that her melancholy voice could compass. It must cease, she must know the truth at whatever cost. He broke through the hedge and stood in the flicker of the moonlight before her, pale, agitated, all unlike his wonted self.

She did not hear, amid the tumult of her weeping, the rustling of the boughs, but some subtle sense took cognizance of his presence. She half rose, and with one hand holding back her dense yellow hair, which had fallen forward on her forehead, she looked up at him fearfully, tremulously, with all the revolt of the corporeal creature for the essence of the mysterious incorporeal. For a moment he could not speak. So much he must needs explain. The next instant he was whelmed in the avalanche of her words.

"Ye hev kem!" she exclaimed in a sort of shrill ecstasy. "Ye hev kem so far ter hear the word that I would give my life ter hev said before. Ye knowed it in heaven! An' how like ye ter kem ter gin me the

WITH ONE HAND HOLDING BACK HER DENSE YELLOW HAIR . . . SHE LOOKED UP AT HIM

chanst ter say it at last! How like the good heart of ye, worth all the hearts on yearth —an' *buried hyar!*"

With her open palm she smote the insensate clods with a gesture of despair. Then she went on in a rising tide of tumultuous emotion. "I love ye! Oh, I *always* loved ye! I never keered fur nobody else! An' I war tongue-tied, an' full of fool pride, an' faultin' ye fur yer ways; an' I wouldn't gin ye the word I knowed ye war wantin' ter hear. But now I kin tell the pore ghost of ye—I kin tell the pore, pore ghost!"

She buried her swollen, tear-stained face in her hands, and shook her head to and fro with the realization of the futility of late repentance. As she once more lifted her eyes, she was obviously surprised to see him still standing there, and the crisis seemed to restore to him the faculty of speech.

"Minta Elladine," he said huskily and prosaically, "I ain't dead!"

She sprang to her feet and stood gazing at him, intent and quivering.

"I be truly alive an' kickin', an' ez worthless ez ever," he went on.

She said not a word, but bent and pallid,

HIS UNQUIET GHOST

and, quaking in every muscle, stood peering beneath her hand, which still held back her hair.

"It's all a mistake," he urged. "This ain't no grave. The top war dug a leetle ter turn off a revenuer's suspicions o' the moonshiners. They put that tale out."

Still, evidently on the verge of collapse, she did not speak.

"Ye needn't be afeared ez I be goin' ter take fur true all I hearn ye say; folks air gin ter vauntin' the dead," he paused for a moment, remembering the caustic comments over the deal of the cards, then added, "though I reckon *I* hev hed some cur'ous 'speriences ez a harnt."

She suddenly threw up both arms with a shrill scream, half nervous exhaustion, half inexpressible delight. She swayed to and fro, almost fainting, her balance failing. He caught her in his arms, and she leaned sobbing against his breast.

"I stand ter every word of it," she cried, her voice broken and lapsed from control. "I love ye, an' I despise all the rest!"

"I be powerful wild," he suggested contritely.

HIS UNQUIET GHOST

"*I* ain't keerin' ef ye be ez wild ez a deer."

"But I'm goin' to quit gamesome company an' playin' kyerds an' sech. I expec' ter mend my ways now," he promised eagerly.

"Ye kin mend 'em or let 'em stay tore, jes ez ye please," she declared recklessly. "I ain't snatched my lovyer from the jaws o' death ter want him otherwise; ye be plumb true-hearted, *I know.*"

"I mought ez well hev been buried in this grave fer the last ten year' fer all the use I hev been," he protested solemnly; "but I hev learnt a lesson through bein' a harnt fer a while—I hev jes kem ter life. I'm goin' ter *live* now. I'll make myself some use in the world, an' fust off I be goin' ter hinder the murder of a man what they hev got trapped up yander at the still."

This initial devoir of his reformation, however, Wyatt found no easy matter. The event had been craftily planned to seem an accident, a fall from a cliff in pursuing the wagon, and only the most ardent and cogent urgency on Wyatt's part prevailed at length. He argued that this interpretation of the disaster would not satisfy the authorities. To take the raider's life insured discovery, retribution. But as he had been brought to the still in the night, it was obvious that if he were conveyed under cover of darkness and by roundabout trails within striking distance of the settlements, he could never again find his way to the locality in the dense wilderness. In his detention he had necessarily learned nothing fresh, for the only names he could have overheard had long been obnoxious to suspicion of moonshining, and afforded no proof. Thus humanity, masquerading as caution, finally triumphed, and the officer, blindfolded, was conducted through devious and winding ways many miles distant, and released within a day's travel of the county town.

Walter Wyatt was scarcely welcomed back to life by the denizens of the cove generally with the enthusiasm attendant on the first moments of his resuscitation, so to speak. He never forgot the solemn ecstasy of that experience, and in later years he was wont to annul any menace of discord with his wife by the warning, half jocose, half tender: "Ye hed better mind; ye'll be sorry some day

HIS UNQUIET GHOST

fur treatin' me so mean. Remember, I hev viewed ye a-weepin' over my grave before now."

A reformation, however complete and salutary, works no change of identity, and although he developed into an orderly, industrious, law-abiding citizen, his prankish temperament remained recognizable in the fantastic fables which he delighted to recount at some genial fireside of what he had seen and heard as a ghost.

" 'Pears like, Watt, ye hed more experiences whenst dead than livin'," said an auditor, as these stories multiplied.

"I did, fur a fack," Watt protested. "I war a powerful onchancy, onquiet ghost. I even did my courtin' whilst in my reg'lar line o' business a-harntin' a graveyard."

A CHILHOWEE LILY

Tall, delicate, and stately, with all the finished symmetry and distinction that might appertain to a cultivated plant, yet sharing that fragility of texture and peculiar suggestion of evanescence characteristic of the unheeded weed as it flowers, the Chilhowee lily caught his eye. Albeit long familiar, the bloom was now invested with a special significance and the sight of it brought him to a sudden pause.

The cluster grew in a niche on the rocky verge of a precipice beetling over the windings of the rugged primitive road on the slope of the ridge. The great pure white bloom, trumpet-shaped and crowned with its flaring and many-cleft paracorolla, distinct against the densely blue sky, seemed the more ethereal because of the delicacy of its stalk, so erect, so inflexibly upright. About it the rocks were at intervals green with moss, and showed here and there heavy ocherous water stain. The luxuriant ferns and pendant vines in the densely umbrageous tangle of verdure served to heighten by con-

A CHILHOWEE LILY

trast the keen whiteness of the flower and the isolation of its situation.

Ozias Crann sighed with perplexity as he looked, and then his eye wandered down the great bosky slope of the wooded mountain where in marshy spots, here and there, a sudden white flare in the shadows betokened the Chilhowee lily, flowering in myraids, holding out lures bewildering in their multitude.

"They air bloomin' bodaciously all over the mounting," he remarked rancorously, as he leaned heavily on a pickaxe; "but we uns hed better try it ter-night ennyhows."

It was late in August; a moon of exceeding lustre was in the sky, while still the sun was going down. All the western clouds were aflare with gorgeous reflections; the long reaches of the Great Smoky range had grown densely purple; and those dim Cumberland heights that, viewed from this precipice of Chilhowee, were wont to show so softly blue in the distance, had now a variant amethystine hue, hard and translucent of effect as the jewel itself.

The face of one of his companions expressed an adverse doubt, as he, too, gazed at the illuminated wilderness, all solitary, silent, remote.

" 'Pears like ter me it mought be powerful public," Pete Swofford objected. He had a tall, heavy, lumpish, frame, a lackluster eye, a broad, dimpled, babyish face incongruously decorated with a tuft of dark beard at the chin. The suit of brown jeans which he wore bore token variously of the storms it had weathered, and his coarse cowhide boots were drawn over the trousers to the knee. His attention was now and again diverted from the conversation by the necessity of aiding a young bear, which he led by a chain, to repel the unwelcome demonstrations of two hounds belonging to one of his interlocutors. Snuffling and nosing about in an affectation of curiosity the dogs could not forbear growling outright, as their muzzles approached their shrinking hereditary enemy, while the cub nestled close to his master and whimpered like a child.

"Jes' so, jes' so, Honey. I'll make 'em cl'ar out!" Swofford replied to the animal's appeal with ready sympathy. Then, "I wish ter Gawd, Rufe, ye'd call yer dogs off," he added in a sort of aside to the youngest of

A CHILHOWEE LILY

the three mountaineers, who stood among the already reddening sumac fringing the road, beside his horse, athwart which lay a buck all gray and antlered, his recently cut throat still dripping blood. The party had been here long enough for it to collect in a tiny pool in a crevice in the rocky road, and the hounds constrained to cease their harassments of the bear now began to eagerly lap it up. The rifle with which Rufe Kinnicutt had killed the deer was still in his hands and he leaned upon it; he was a tall, finely formed, athletic young fellow with dark hair, keen, darkly greenish eyes, full of quickly glancing lights, and as he, too, scanned the sky, his attitude of mind also seemed dissuasive.

" 'Pears like thar won't be no night, ez ye mought call night, till this moon goes down," he suggested. " 'Pears nigh ez bright ez day!"

Ozias Crann's lank, angular frame; his narrow, bony face; his nose, long yet not large, sharp, pinched; his light grey eyes, set very closely together; his straggling reddish beard, all were fitting concomitants to accent the degree of caustic contempt he expressed. "Oh, to be sure!" he drawled. "It'll be powerful public up hyar in the mounting in the midnight,—that's a fac'!—an' moonlight is mighty illconvenient to them ez wants ter git spied on through totin' a lantern in cur'ous places."

This sarcasm left the two remonstrants out of countenance. Pete Swofford found a certain resource in the agitations of his bear, once more shrinking and protesting because of the dogs. "Call off yer hound-dogs, Rufe," he cried irritably, "or I'll gin 'em a bullet ter swallow."

"Ye air a plumb fool about that thar bar, Pete," Kinnicutt said sourly, calling off the hounds nevertheless.

"That thar bar?" exclaimed Swofford. "Why, thar never war sech a bar! That thar bar goes ter mill, an' kin fetch home grist,—ef I starts him out in the woods whar he won't meet no dogs nor contrairy cattle o' men he kin go ter mill all by his lone!— same ez folks an' the bes' kind o' folks, too!"

In fact the bear was even now begirt with a meal-bag, well filled, which although adding to his uncouth appearance and perhaps un-

A CHILHOWEE LILY

duly afflicting the sensibilities of the horse, who snorted and reared at the sight of him, saved his master the labor of "packing" the heavy weight.

Swofford had his genial instincts and in return was willing to put up with the cubbishness of the transport,—would wait in the illimitable patience of the utterly idle for the bear to climb a tree if he liked and pleasantly share with him the persimmons of his quest; —would never interfere when the bear flung himself down and wallowed with the bag on his back, and would reply to the censorious at home, objecting to the dust and sand thus sifting in with the meal, with the time honored reminder that we are all destined "to eat a peck of dirt" in this world.

"Whenst ye fust spoke o' diggin'," said Kinnicutt, interrupting a lengthening account of the bear's mental and moral graces, "I 'lowed ez ye mought be sayin' ez they air layin' off ter work agin in the Tanglefoot Mine."

Ozias Crann lifted a scornful chin. "I reckon the last disasters thar hev interrupted the company so ez they hain't got much heart todes diggin' fur silver agin over in Tangle-

A CHILHOWEE LILY

foot Cove. Fust," he checked off these misfortunes, by laying the fingers of one hand successively in the palm of the other, "the timbers o' one o' the cross cuts fell an' the roof caved in an' them two men war kilt, an' thar famblies sued the company an' got mo' damages 'n the men war bodaciously wuth. Then the nex' thing the pay agent, ez war sent from Glaston, war held up in Tanglefoot an' robbed—some say by the miners. He got hyar whenst they war out on a strike, an' they robbed him 'cause they warn't paid cordin' ter thar lights, an' they *did* shoot him up cornsider'ble. That happened jes' about a year ago. Then sence, thar hev been a awful cavin' in that deep shaft they hed sunk in the tunnel, an' the mine war flooded an' the machinery ruint—I reckon the company in Glaston ain't a-layin' off ter fly in the face o' Providence and begin agin, arter all them leadin's ter quit."

"Some believe he warn't robbed at all," Kinnicutt said slowly. He had turned listlessly away, evidently meditating departure, his hand on his horse's mane, one foot in the stirrup.

"Ye know that gal named Loralindy Byars?" Crann said craftily.

A CHILHOWEE LILY

Kinnicutt paused abruptly. Then as the schemer remained silent he demanded, frowning darkly, "What's Loralindy Byars got ter do with it?"

"Mighty nigh all!" Crann exclaimed, triumphantly.

It was a moment of tense suspense. But it was not Crann's policy to tantalize him further, however much the process might address itself to his peculiar interpretation of pleasure. "That thar pay agent o' the mining company," he explained, "he hed some sort'n comical name—oh, I remember now, Renfrow—Paul Renfrow—waal—ye know he war shot in the knee when the miners way-laid him."

"I disremember now ef it war in the knee or the thigh," Swofford interposed, heavily pondering.

Kinnicutt's brow contracted angrily, and Crann broke into open wrath: "An' I ain't carin', ye fool—what d' ye interrupt fur like that?"

"Wall," protested Swofford, indignantly, "ye said 'ye know' an' I didn't *know*."

"An' I aint carin'—the main p'int war that he could neither ride nor walk. So the critter crawled! Nobody knows how he gin the strikers the slip, but he got through ter old man Byars's house. An' thar he staid till Loralindy an' the old 'oman Byars nussed him up so ez he could bear the pain o' bein' moved. An' he got old man Byars ter wagin him down ter Colb'ry, a-layin' on two feather beds 'count o' the rocky roads, an' thar he got on the steam kyars an' he rid on them back ter whar he kem from."

Kinnicutt seemed unable to longer restrain his impatience. He advanced a pace. "Ye appear ter 'low ez ye air tellin' news— I knowed all that whenst it happened a full year ago!"

"I reckon ye know, too, ez Loralindy hed no eyes nor ears fur ennybody else whilst he war hyar—but then *he war* good-lookin' an' saaft-spoken fur true! An' now he hev writ a letter ter her!"

Crann grinned as Kinnicutt inadvertently gasped. "How do you uns know that?" the young man hoarsely demanded, with a challenging accent of doubt, yet prescient despair.

" 'Kase, bubby, that's the way the story 'bout the lily got out. I was at the mill this

A CHILHOWEE LILY

actial day. The miller hed got the letter—hevin' been ter the post-office at the Crossroads—an' he read it ter her, bein' ez Loralindy can't read writin'. She warn't expectin' it. He writ of his own accord."

A sense of shadows impended vaguely over all the illuminated world, and now and again a flicker of wings through the upper atmosphere betokened the flight of homing birds. Crann gazed about him absently while he permitted the statement he had made to sink deep into the jealous, shrinking heart of the young mountaineer, and he repeated it as he resumed.

"She warnt' expectin' of the letter. She jes' stood thar by the mill-door straight an' slim an' white an' still, like she always be—ter my mind like she war some sort'n sperit, stiddier a sure enough gal—with her yaller hair slick an' plain, an' that old, faded, green cotton dress she mos' always wears, an' lookin' quiet out at the water o' the mill-dam ter one side, with the trees a-wavin' behind her at the open door—jes' like she always be! An' arter awhile she speaks slow an' saaft an axes the miller ter read it aloud ter her. An' lo! old man Bates war rej'iced an' glorified ter the bone ter be able ter git a peck inter that letter! He jes' shet down the gates and stopped the mill from runnin' in a jiffy, an' tole all them loafers, ez hangs round thar mos'ly, ter quit thar noise. An' then he propped hisself up on a pile o' grist, an' thar he read all the sayin's ez war writ in that letter. An' a power o' time it tuk, an' a power o' spellin' an' bodaciously wrastlin' with the alphabit."

He laughed lazily, as he turned his quid of tobacco in his mouth, recollecting the turbulence of these linguistic turmoils.

"This hyar feller—this Renfrow—he called her in the letter 'My dear friend'— he did—an' 'lowed he hed a right ter the word, fur ef ever a man war befriended he hed been. He 'lowed ez he could never furget her. An' Lord! how it tickled old man Bates ter read them sentiments—the prideful old peacock! He would jes' stop an' push his spectacles back on his slick bald head an' say, 'Ye hear me, Loralindy! he 'lows he'll never furget the keer ye tuk o' him whenst he war shot an' ailin' an' nigh ter death. An' no mo' he ought, nuther. But some do furget sech ez that, Loralindy—some do!'

A CHILHOWEE LILY

An' them fellers at the mill, listenin' ter the letter, could sca'cely git thar consent ter wait fur old man Bates ter git through his talk ter Loralindy, that he kin talk ter every day in the year! But arter awhile he settled his spectacles agin, an' tuk another tussle with the spellin,' an' then he rips out the main p'int o' the letter. This stranger-man he 'lowed he war bold enough ter ax another favior. The cuss tried ter be funny. 'One good turn desarves another,' he said. 'An' ez ye hev done me one good turn, I want ye ter do me another.' An' old man Bates hed the insurance ter waste the time a-laffin' an' a-laffin' at sech a good joke. Them fellers at the mill could hev fund it in thar hearts ter grind him up in his own hopper, ef it wouldn't hev ground up with him thar chance o' ever hearin' the e-end o' that thar interestin' letter. So thar comes the favior. Would she dig up that box he treasured from whar he told her he hed buried it, arter he escaped from the attack o' the miners? An' would she take the box ter Colb'ry in her grandad's wagin, an' send it ter him by express. He hed tole her once whar he hed placed it—an' ter mark the spot mo' per-

A CHILHOWEE LILY

cisely he hed noticed one Chilhowee lily bulb right beside it. An' then says the letter, 'Good bye, Chilhowee Lily!' An' all them fellers stood staring."

A light wind was under way from the west. Delicate flakes of red and glistening white were detached from the clouds. Sails—sails were unfurling in the vast floods of the skies. With flaunting banners and swelling canvas a splendid fleet reached half way to the zenith. But a more multitudinous shipping still swung at anchor low in the west, though the promise of a fair night as yet held fast.

"An' now," said Ozias Crann in conclusion, "all them fellers is a-diggin'."

"Whut's in the box?" demanded Swofford, his big baby-face all in a pucker of doubt.

"The gold an' silver he ought ter hev paid the miners, of course. They always 'lowed they never tuk a dollar off him; they jes' got a long range shot at him! How I wish," Ozias Crann broke off fervently, "how I wish I could jes' git my hands on that money once!" He held out his hands, long and sinewy, and opened and shut them very fast.

A CHILHOWEE LILY

"Why, that would be stealin'!" exclaimed Kinnicutt with repulsion.

"How so? 't ain't his'n now, sure—he war jes' the agent ter pay it out," argued Crann, volubly.

"It belongs ter the mine owners, then—the company." There was a suggestion of inquiry in the younger man's tone.

" 'Pears not—they sent it hyar fur the percise purpose ter be paid out!" the specious Crann replied.

"Then it belongs ter the miners."

"They hedn't yearned it—an' ef some o' them hed they warn't thar ter receive it, bein' out on a strike. They hed burnt down the company's office over yander at the mine in Tanglefoot Cove, with all the books an' accounts, an' now nobody knows what's owin' ter who."

Kinnicutt's moral protests were silenced, not satisfied. He looked up moodily at the moon now alone in the sky, for only a vanishing segment of the great vermilion sphere of the sun was visible above the western mountains, when suddenly he felt one of those long grasping claws on his arm. "Now, Rufe,

A CHILHOWEE LILY

bubby," a most insinuating tone, Crann had summoned, "all them fool fellers air diggin' up the face of the yearth, wharever they kin find a Chilhowee lily—like sarchin' fur a needle in a haystack. But we uns will do a better thing than that. I drawed the idee ez soon ez I seen you an' Pete hyar this evenin' so onexpected. 'Them's my pardners,' I sez ter myself. 'Pete ter holp dig an' tote ef the box be heavy. An' you ter find out edzac'ly whar it be hid.' You uns an' Loralindy hev been keepin' company right smart, an' ye kin toll Loralindy along till she lets slip jes' whar that lily air growin'. I'll be bound ez she likes ye a sight better 'n that Renfrow— leastwise ef 't warn't fur his letter, honeyin' her up with complimints, an' she hevin' the chance o' tollin' him on through doin' him sech faviors, savin' his life, an' now his money—shucks it's mo' *our* money 'n his'n; 't ain't his'n! Gol-darn the insurance o' this Renfrow! His idee is ter keep the money his own self, an' make her sen' it ter him. Then 'Good-bye, Chilhowee Lily!' "

The night had come at last, albeit almost as bright as day, but with so ethereal, so chastened a splendor that naught of day

A CHILHOWEE LILY

seemed real. A world of dreams it was, of gracious illusions, of far vague distances that lured with fair promises that the eye might not seek to measure. The gorgeous tints were gone, and in their stead were soft grays and indefinite blurring browns, and every suggestion of silver that metal can show flashed in variant glitter in the moon. The mountains were majestically sombre, with a mysterious sense of awe in their great height. There were few stars; only here and there the intense lustre of a still planet might withstand the annihilating magnificence of the moon.

Its glamour did not disdain the embellishment of humbler objects. As Rufe Kinnicutt approached a little log cabin nestling in a sheltered cove he realized that a year had gone by since Renfrow had seen it first, and that thus it must have appeared when he beheld it. The dew was bright on the slanting roof, and the shadow of oak trees wavered over it. The mountain loomed above. The zigzag lines of the rail fence, the beegums all awry ranged against it, the rickety barn and fowl-house, the gourd vines draping the porch of the dwelling, all had a glimmer

A CHILHOWEE LILY

of dew and a picturesque symmetry, while the spinning wheel as Loralinda sat in the white effulgent glow seemed to revolve with flashes of light in lieu of spokes, and the thread she drew forth was as silver. Its murmuring rune was hardly distinguishable from the chant of the cicada or the long droning in strophe and antistrophe of the waterside frogs far away, but such was the whir or her absorption that she did not perceive his approach till his shadow fell athwart the threshold, and she looked up with a start.

"Ye 'pear powerful busy a-workin' hyar so late in the night," he exclaimed with a jocose intonation.

She smiled, a trifle abashed; then evidently conscious of the bizarre suggestions of so much ill-timed industry, she explained, softly drawling: "Waal, ye know, Granny, she be so harried with her rheumatics ez she gits along powerful poor with her wheel, an' by night she be plumb out'n heart an' mad fur true. So arter she goes ter bed I jes' spins a passel fur her, an' nex' mornin' she 'lows she done a toler'ble stint o' work an' air consider'ble s'prised ez she war so easy put out."

A CHILHOWEE LILY

She laughed a little, but he did not respond. With his sensibilities all jarred by the perfidious insinuation of Ozias Crann, and his jealousy all on the alert, he noted and resented the fact that at first her attention had come back reluctantly to him, and that he, standing before her, had been for a moment a less definitely realized presence than the thought in her mind—this thought had naught to do with him, and of that he was sure.

"Loralindy," he said with a turbulent impulse of rage and grief; "whenst ye promised to marry me ye an' me war agreed that we would never hev one thought hid from one another—ain't that a true word?"

The wheel had stopped suddenly—the silver thread was broken; she was looking up at him, the moonlight full on the straight delicate lineaments of her pale face, and the smooth glister of her golden hair. "Not o' my own," she stipulated. And he remembered, and wondered that it should come to him so late, that she had stood upon this reservation and that he—poor fool—had conceded it, thinking it concerned the distilling of whisky in defiance of the revenue law, in which some of her relatives were suspected to be engaged, and of which he wished to know as little as possible.

The discovery of his fatuity was not of soothing effect. " 'T war that man Renfrow's secret—I hearn about his letter what war read down ter the mill."

She nodded acquiescently, her expression once more abstracted, her thoughts far afield.

He had one moment of triumph as he brought himself tensely erect, shouldering his gun—his shadow behind him in the moonlight duplicated the gesture with a sharp promptness as at a word of command.

"All the mounting's a-diggin' by this time!" He laughed with ready scorn, then experienced a sudden revulsion of feeling. Her face had changed. Her expression was unfamiliar. She had caught together the two ends of the broken thread, and was knotting them with a steady hand, and a look of composed security on her face, that was itself a flout to the inopportune search of the mountaineers and boded ill to his hope to discover from her the secret of the *cache*. He recovered himself suddenly.

"Ye 'lowed ter me ez ye never keered

A CHILHOWEE LILY

nuthin' fur that man, Renfrow,'' he said with a plaintive appeal, far more powerful with her than scorn.

She looked up at him with candid reassuring eyes. "I never keered none fur him," she protested. "He kem hyar all shot up, with the miners an' mounting boys hot foot arter him—an' we done what we could fur him. Gran'daddy 'lowed ez *he* warn't 'sponsible fur whut the owners done, or hedn't done at the mine, an' he seen no sense in shootin' one man ter git even with another."

"But ye kep' his secret!" Kinnicutt persisted.

"What fur should I tell it—'t ain't mine?"

"That thar money in that box he buried ain't *his'n*, nuther!" he argued.

There was an inscrutable look in her clear eyes. She had risen, and was standing in the moonlight opposite him. The shadows of the vines falling over her straight skirt left her face and hair the fairer in the silver glister.

" 'Pears like ter me," he broke the silence with his plaintive cadence, "ez ye ought ter hev tole me. I ain't keerin' ter know 'ceptin' ye hev shet me out. It hev hurt my feelin's powerful ter be treated that-a-way. Tell me now—or lemme go forever!"

She was suddenly trembling from head to foot. Pale she was always. Now she was ghastly. "Rufe Kinnicutt," she said with the solemnity of an adjuration, "ye don't keer fur sech ez this, fur *nuthin'*. An' I promised!"

He noted her agitation. He felt the clue in his grasp. He sought to wield his power, "Choose a-twixt us! Choose a-twixt the promise ye made ter that man—or the word ye deny ter me! An' when I'm gone—I'm gone!"

She stood seemingly irresolute.

"It's nuthin' ter me," he protested once more. "I kin keep it an' gyard it ez well ez you uns. But I won't be shet out, an' doubted, an' denied, like ez ef *I* wan't fitten ter be trested with nuthin'!"

He stood a moment longer, watching her trembling agitation, and feeling that tingling exasperation that might have preceded a blow.

"I'm goin'," he threatened.

As she still stood motionless he turned

A CHILHOWEE LILY

away as if to make good his threat. He heard a vague stir among the leaves, and turning back he saw that the porch was vacant.

He had overshot the mark. In swift repentance he retraced his steps. He called her name. No response save the echoes. The house dogs, roused to a fresh excitement, were gathering about the door, barking in affected alarm, save one, to whom Kinnicutt was a stranger, that came, silent and ominous, dragging a block and chain from under the house. Kinnicutt heard the sudden drowsy plaints of the old rheumatic grandmother, as she was rudely awakened by the clamors, and presently a heavy footfall smote upon the puncheons that floored the porch. Old Byars himself, with his cracked voice and long gray hair, had left his pipe on the mantel-piece to investigate the disorder without.

"Hy're Rufe!" he swung uneasily posed on his crutch stick in the doorway, and mechanically shaded his eyes with one hand, as from the sun, as he gazed dubiously at the young man, "hain't ye in an' about finished yer visit?—or yer visitation, ez the

A CHILHOWEE LILY

pa'son calls it. He, he, he! Wall, Loralindy hev gone up steers ter the roof-room, an' it's about time ter bar up the doors. Waal, joy go with ye, he, he, he! Come off, Tige, *ye* Bose, hyar! Cur'ous I can't l'arn them dogs no manners.''

A dreary morrow ensued on the splendid night. The world was full of mists; the clouds were resolved into drizzling rain; every perspective of expectation was restricted by the limited purlieus of the present. The treasure-seekers digging here and there throughout the forest in every nook in low ground, wherever a drift of the snowy blossoms might glimmer, began to lose hope and faith. Now and again some iconoclastic soul sought to stigmatize the whole rumor as a fable. More than one visited the Byars cabin in the desperate hope that some chance word might fall from the girl, giving a clue to the mystery.

By daylight the dreary little hut had no longer poetic or picturesque suggestion. Bereft of the sheen and shimmer of the moonlight its aspect had collapsed like a dream into the dullest realities. The door-yard was muddy and littered; here the razor-back hogs

A CHILHOWEE LILY

rooted unrebuked; the rail fence had fallen on one side, and it would seem that only their attachment to home prevented them from wandering forth to be lost in the wilderness; the clap-boards of the shiny roof were oozing and steaming with dampness, and showed all awry and uneven; the clay and stick chimney, hopelessly out of plumb, leaned far from the wall.

Within it was not more cheerful; the fire smoked gustily into the dim little room, illumined only by the flicker of the blaze and the discouraged daylight from the open door, for the batten shutters of the unglazed window were closed. The puncheon floor was grimy—the feet that curiosity had led hither brought much red clay mire upon them. The poultry, all wet and dispirited, ventured within and stood about the door, now scuttling in sudden panic and with peevish squawks upon the unexpected approach of a heavy foot. Loralinda, sitting at her spinning wheel, was paler than ever, all her dearest illusions dashed into hopeless fragments, and a promise which she did not value to one whom she did not love quite perfect and intact.

A CHILHOWEE LILY

The venerable grandmother sat propped with pillows in her arm-chair, and now and again adjured the girl to "show some manners an' tell the neighbors what they so honed to know." With the vehemence of her insistence her small wizened face would suddenly contract; the tortures of the rheumatism, particularly rife in such weather, would seize upon her, and she would cry aloud with anguish, and clutch her stick and smite her granddaughter to expedite the search for the primitive remedies of dried "yarbs" on which her comfort depended.

"Oh, Lord!" she would wail as she fell back among the pillows. "I'm a-losin' all my religion amongst these hyar rheumatics. I wish I war a man jes' ter say 'damn 'em' once! An' come good weather I'll sca'cely be able ter look Loralindy in the face, considerin' how I hector her whilst I be in the grip o' this misery."

"Jes' pound away, Granny, ef it makes ye feel ennywise better," cried Loralinda, furtively rubbing the weales on her arm. "It don't hurt me wuth talkin' 'bout. Ye jes' pound away, an' welcome!"

Perhaps it was her slender, elastic

strength and erect grace, with her shining hair and ethereal calm pallor in the midst of the storm that evoked the comparison, for Ozias Crann was suddenly reminded of the happy similitude suggested by the letter that he had heard read and had repeated yesterday to his cronies as he stood in the road. The place was before him for one illumined moment—the niche in the cliff, with its ferns and vines, the delicate stately dignity of the lilies outlined against the intense blue of the sky.

The reminiscence struck him like a discovery. Where else could the flower have been so naturally noticed by this man, a stranger, and remembered as a mark in the expectation of finding it once more when the bulb should flower again—as beside the county road? He would have been hopelessly lost a furlong from the path.

Crann stood for a moment irresolute, then silently grasped his pickaxe and slunk out among the mists on the porch.

He berated his slow mind as he hurried invisible through the vast clouds in which the world seemed lost. Why should the laggard inspiration come so late if it had come

A CHILHOWEE LILY

at all? Why should he, with the clue lying half developed in his own mental impressions, have lost all the vacant hours of the long, bright night, have given the rumor time to pervade the mountains, and set all the idlers astir before he should strike the decisive blow?

There, at last, was the cliff, beetling far over the mist-filled valley below. A slant of sunshine fell on the surging vapor, and it gleamed opalescent. There was the niche, with the lilies all a-bloom. He came panting up the slope under the dripping trees, with a dash of wind in his face and the odor of damp leafage and mold on the freshening air.

He struck the decisive blow with a will. The lilies shivered and fell apart. The echoes multiplied the stroke with a ringing metallic iteration.

The loiterers were indeed abroad. The sound lured them from their own devious points of search, and a half dozen of the treasure-seekers burst from the invisibilities of the mists as Ozias Crann's pickaxe cleaving the mold struck upon the edge of a small japanned box hidden securely between the

A CHILHOWEE LILY

rocks, a scant foot below the surface. A dangerous spot for a struggle, the verge of a precipice, but the greed for gain is a passion that blunts the sense of peril. The wrestling figures, heedless of the abyss, swayed hither and thither, the precious box among them; now it was captured by a stronger grasp, now secured anew by sheer sleight-of-hand. More than once it dropped to the ground, and at last in falling the lock gave way, and scattered to the wind were numberless orderly vouchers for money already paid, inventories of fixtures, bills for repairs, reports of departments—various details of value in settling the accounts of the mine, and therefore to be transmitted to the main office of the mining company at Glaston.

"Ef I hed tole ye ez the money warn't thar, ye wouldn't hev believed me," Loralinda Byars said drearily, when certain disappointed wights, who had sought elsewhere and far a-field, repaired to the cabin laughing at their own plight and upbraiding her with the paucity of the *cache*. "I knowed all the time what war in that box. The man lef' it thar in the niche arter he war shot, it bein' heavy ter tote an' not wuth much. But he

A CHILHOWEE LILY

brung the money with him, an' tuk it off, bein', he said, without orders from the owners, the miners hevin' burnt down the offices, an' bruk open the safe an' destroyed all the papers, ceptin' that leetle box. I sewed up the man's money myself in them feather beds what he lay on whenst he war wagined down 'ter Colb'ry ter take the kyars. He 'lowed the compn'y mought want them papers whenst they went into liquidation, ez he called it, an' tole me how he hed hid 'em.''

Rufe Kinnicutt wondered that she should have been so unyielding. She did not speculate on the significance of her promise. She did not appraise its relative value with other interests, and seek to qualify it. Once given she simply kept it. She held herself no free agent. It was not hers.

The discovery that the lure was gold revealed the incentive of her lover's jealous demand to share the custody of the secret. His intention was substituted for the deed in her rigid interpretation of integrity. It cost her many tears. But she seemed thereafter to him still more unyielding, as erect, fragile, ethereally pure and pale she noted his passing no more than the lily might. He

A CHILHOWEE LILY

often thought of the cheap lure of the sophisms that had so deluded him, the simple obvious significance of the letter, and the phrase, "Goodbye, Chilhowee Lily," had also an echo of finality for him.

THE PHANTOM OF BOGUE HOLAUBA

Gordon never forgot the sensation he experienced on first beholding it. There was no mist in the midnight. The moon was large and low. The darkness of the dense, towering forests on either hand impinged in no wise on the melancholy realm of wan light in which the Mississippi lay, unshadowed, solitary, silent as always, its channel here a mile or more in breadth.

He had been observing how the mighty water-course was sending out its currents into a bayou, called Bogue Holauba, as if the larger stream were a tributary of the lesser. This peculiarity of the river in the deltaic region, to throw off volume instead of continually receiving affluents, was unaccustomed to him, being a stranger to the locality, and for a moment it focussed his interest. The next, his every faculty was concentrated on a singular phenomenon on the bank of the bogue.

He caught his breath with a gasp; then, without conscious volition, he sought to ex-

THE PHANTOM OF BOGUE HOLAUBA

plain it to his own shocked senses, to realize it as some illusion, some combination of natural causes, the hour, the pallor pervading the air, the distance, for his boat was near the middle of the stream,—but the definiteness of the vision annulled his efforts.

There on the broad, low margin, distinct, yet with a coercive conviction of unreality, the figure of a man drawn in lines of vague light paced slowly to and fro; an old man, he would have said, bent and wizened, swaying back and forth, in expressive contortions, a very pantomime of woe, wringing gaunt hands and arms above his head, and now and again bowing low in recurrent paroxysms of despair. The wind held its breath, and the river, mute as ever, made no sign, and the encompassing alluvial wilderness stood for a type of solitude. Only the splashing of the paddle of the "dug-out" gave token of the presence of life in all the land.

Gordon could not restrain his wonder. "What—what—is—that Thing—over there on the bank of the bogue?" he called out to the negro servant who was paddling the canoe.

He was all unprepared for the effect of

THE PHANTOM OF BOGUE HOLAUBA

his words. Indeed, he was fain to hold hard to the gunwales. For the negro, with a sudden galvanic start, let slip the paddle from his hand, recovering it only by a mighty lunge in a mechanical impulse of self-preservation. The dug-out, the most tricksy craft afloat, rocked violently in the commotion and threatened to capsize. Then, as it finally righted, its course was hastily changed, and under the impetus of panic terror it went shooting down the river at a tremendous speed.

"Why, what does all this mean?" demanded Gordon.

"Don't ye talk ter me, boss!" the boatman, with chattering teeth, adjured his passenger. "Don't ye talk ter me, boss! Don't tell me ye seed somepin over dar on Bogue Holauba—'kase ef ye *do* I'se gwine ter turn dis dug-out upside down an' swim out ter de Arkansas side. I ain't gwine ter paddle dis boat fur no ghost-seer, sure 's ye are born. I ain't gwine ter have no traffickin' wid ghosts nur ghost-seers nuther. I'd die 'fore de year's out, sure!"

The sincerity of the servant's fright was attested by the change in his manner. He had been hitherto all cheerful, though respectful, affability, evidently bidding high for a tip. Now he crouched disconsolate and sullen in his place, wielding the paddle with all his might, and sedulously holding down his head, avoiding the stranger's eye.

Gordon felt the whole situation in some sort an affront to his dignity, and the apparition being withdrawn from view by the changed direction, he was in better case to take account of this,—to revolt at the uncouth character of the craft and guide sent for him; the absence of any member of his entertainer's family to welcome the visitor, here at their instance and invitation; the hour of the night; the uncanny incident of the inexplicable apparition,—but when that thought recurred to him he sheered off precipitately from the recollection.

It had the salutary effect of predisposing him to make the best of the situation. Being to a degree a man of the world and of a somewhat large experience, he began to argue within himself that he could scarcely have expected a different reception in these conditions. The great river being at the stage known as "dead low water," steamboat travel was practically suspended for the season, or he could have reached his destination more directly than by rail. An accident had delayed the train some seven hours, and although the gasoline launch sent to meet him at the nearest way-station had been withdrawn at nightfall, since he did not arrive, as his sable attendant informed him, the dug-out had been substituted, with instructions to wait all night, on the remote chance that he might come, after all.

Nevertheless, it was with an averse, disaffected gaze that he silently watched the summit-line of foliage on either bank of the river glide slowly along the sky, responsive to the motion of the boat. It seemed a long monotony of this experience, as he sat listless in the canoe, before a dim whiteness began to appear in a great, unbroken expanse in the gradually enlarging riparian view— the glister of the moon on the open cottonbolls in the fields. The forests were giving way, the region of swamp and bayou. The habitations of man were at hand, and when at last the dug-out was run in to a plantation landing, and Kenneth Gordon was released from his cramped posture in that plebeian craft, he felt so averse to his mission, such a frivolous, reluctant distaste that he marvelled how he was to go through with it at all, as he took his way along the serpentine curves of the "dirt road," preceded by his guide, still with eyes averted and sullen mien, silently bearing his suit-case.

A few turns, and suddenly a large house came into view, rearing its white facade to the moonlight in the midst of a grove of magnolia trees, immense of growth, the glossy leaves seeming a-drip with lùstre as with dew. The flight of steps and the wide veranda were here cumbered with potted ferns and foliage plants as elsewhere, and gave the first suggestion of conformity to the ways of the world that the adventure had yet borne. The long, broad, silent hall into which he was ushered, lighted only by a kerosene hand-lamp which the servant carried as he led the way, the stairs which the guest ascended in a mansion of unconscious strangers, all had eerie intimations, and the comfort and seclusion of the room assigned to Gordon was welcome indeed to him; for, argue as he might, he was conscious of a continuous and acute nervous strain. He had had a shock, he was irritably aware, and he would be glad of rest and quiet.

It was a large, square, comfortable room in one of the wings, overlooking a garden, which sent up a delectable blend of fragrance and dew through the white muslin curtains at the long, broad windows, standing open to the night. On a table, draped with the inevitable "drawn-work" of civilization, stood a lamp of finer fashion, but no better illuminating facilities, than the one carried off by the darky, who had made great haste to leave the room, and who had not lifted his eyes toward the ill-omened "ghost-seer" nor spoken a word since Gordon had blurted out his vision on Bogue Holauba. This table also bore a tray with crackers and sandwiches and a decanter of sherry, which genially intimated hospitable forethought. The bed was a big four-poster, which no bedizenment could bring within the fashion of the day. Gordon had a moment's poignant recoil from the darkness, the strangeness, the recollection of the inexplicable apparition he had witnessed, as his head sank on the pillow, embroidered after the latest fads.

He could see through the open window

that the moon was down at last and the world abandoned to gloom. He heard from out some neighboring swamp the wild lamenting cry of the crane; and then, listen as he might, the night had lapsed to silence, and the human hearts in this house, all unknown to him, were as unimagined, as unrelated, as unresponsive, as if instead of a living, breathing home he lay in some mute city of the dead.

The next moment, as it seemed, a sky as richly azure as the boasted heavens of Italy filled his vision as he lifted himself on his elbow. A splendid, creamy, magnolia bloom was swaying in the breeze, almost touching the window-sill. There was a subdued, respectful knocking at the door, which Gordon had a vague idea that he had heard before this morning, preceding the announcement that breakfast was waiting. Tardily mindful of his obligations as guest, he made all the speed possible in his toilet, and soon issued into the hall, following the sound of voices through the open doors, which led him presently to the threshold of the breakfast-room.

There were two ladies at the table, one of venerable aspect, with short, white curls, held from her face by side-combs, a modish breakfast-cap, and a morning-gown of thin gray silk. The other was young enough to be her daughter, as indeed she was, dressed in deep mourning. Rising instantly from her place as hostess behind the silver service, she extended her hand to the stranger.

"Mr. Gordon, is it not? I was afraid you would arrive during the night. Mercy! So uncomfortable! How good of you to come—yes, indeed."

She sank into her chair again, pressing her black-bordered handkerchief to her dark eyes, which seemed to Gordon singularly dry, round, and glossy—suggestive of chestnuts, in fact. "So good of you to come," she repeated, "to the house of mourning! Very few people have any talent for woe, Mr. Gordon. These rooms have housed many guests, but not to weep with us. The stricken deer must weep alone."

She fell to hysterical sobbing, which her mother interrupted by a remonstrant "My dear, my dear!" A blond young man with a florid cheek and a laughing blue eye, who sat in an easy posture at the foot of the table, aided the diversion of interest. "Won't you introduce me, Mrs. Keene?—or must I take the opportunity to tell Mr. Gordon that I am Dr. Rigdon, very much at his service."

"Mercy! yes, yes, indeed!" Mrs. Keene acceded as the two young men shook hands; then, evidently perturbed by her lack of ceremony, she exclaimed pettishly, "Where is Geraldine? She always sees to it that everybody knows everybody, and that everybody is served at a reception or a tea. I never have to think of such things if *she* is in the house."

The allusions seemed to Gordon a bit incongruous with the recent heavy affliction of the household. The accuracy with which the waves of red hair, of a rich tint that suggested chemicals, undulated about the brow of the widow, the art with which the mourning-gown brought out all the best points and subdued the defects of a somewhat clumsy figure, the suspicion of a cosmetic's aid in a dark line, scarcely perceptible yet amply effective, under the prominent eyes, all contributed to the determination of a lady of forty-five years of age to look thirty.

"Geraldine is always late for breakfast, but surely she ought to be down by this time," Mrs. Brinn said, with as much acrimony as a mild old lady could well compass.

"Oh, Geraldine reads half the night," explained Mrs. Keene. "Such an injurious habit! Don't you think so, Mr. Gordon?"

"Oh, *she* is all right," expostulated the young physician.

"Geraldine has a constitution of iron, I know," Mrs. Keene admitted. "But, mercy! —to live in books, Mr. Gordon. Now, *I* always wanted to live in life,—in the world! I used to tell Mr. Keene"—even she stumbled a trifle in naming the so recent dead. "I used to tell him that he had buried the best years of my life down here in the swamp on the plantation."

"Pleasant for Mr. Keene," Gordon thought.

"I wanted to live in life," reiterated Mrs. Keene. "What is a glimpse of New Orleans or the White Sulphur Springs once in a great while!"

" 'This world is but a fleeting show,' " quoted Rigdon, with a palpable effort to laugh off the inappropriate subject.

"Oh, that is what people always tell the restricted, especially when they are themselves drinking the wine-cup to the bottom."

THE PHANTOM OF BOGUE HOLAUBA

"And finding the lees bitter," said Rigdon.

The widow gave an offhand gesture. "You learned that argument from Geraldine —he is nothing but an echo of Geraldine, Mr. Gordon—now, isn't he, Mamma?" she appealed directly to Mrs. Brinn.

"He seems to have a great respect for Geraldine's opinion," said Mrs. Brinn primly.

"If I may ask, who is this lady who seems to give the law to the community?" inquired Gordon, thinking it appropriate to show, and really beginning to feel, an interest in the personnel of the entourage. "Am I related to her, as well as to Mr. Keene?"

"No; Geraldine is one of the Norris family—intimate friends of ours, but not relatives. She often visits here, and in my affliction and loneliness I begged her to come and stay for several weeks."

Not to be related to the all-powerful Geraldine was something of a disappointment, for although Gordon had little sentiment or ideality in his mental and moral system, one of his few emotional susceptibilities lay in his family pride and clannish spirit. He felt for his own, and he was touched in his chief altruistic possibility in the appeal that had brought him hither. To his amazement, Mr. Keene, a second cousin whom he had seldom even seen, had named him executor of his will, without bond, and in a letter written in the last illness, reaching its destination indeed after the writer's death, had besought that Gordon would be gracious enough to act, striking a crafty note in urging the ties of consanguinity.

But for this plea Gordon would have doubtless declined on the score of pressure of business of his own. There were no nearer relatives, however, and with a sense of obligation at war with a restive indisposition, Gordon had come in person to this remote region to offer the will for probate, and to take charge of the important papers and personal property of the deceased. A simple matter it would prove, he fancied. There was no great estate, and probably but few business complications.

"Going home, Dr. George?" his hostess asked as the young physician made his excuses for quitting the table before the conclusion of the meal.

"Dr. Rigdon is not staying in the house, then?" Gordon queried as the door closed upon him, addressing the remark to the old lady by way of politely including her in the conversation.

"No, he is a neighbor of ours—a close and constant friend to us." Mrs. Brinn spoke as with grateful appreciation.

Mrs. Keene took a different view. "He just hangs about here on Geraldine's account," she said. "He happens to be here to-day because last night she took a notion that he must go all the way to Bogue Holauba to meet you, if the train should stop at the station above; but he was called off to attend a severe case of ptomaine poisoning."

"And did the man die?" Mrs. Brinn asked, with a sort of soft awe.

"Mercy! I declare I forgot to ask him if the man died or not," exclaimed Mrs. Keene. "But that was the reason that only a servant was sent to meet you, Mr. Gordon. The doctor looked in this morning to learn if you had arrived safely, and we made him stay to breakfast with us."

Gordon was regretting that he had let him depart so suddenly.

"I thought perhaps, as he seems so familiar with the place he might show me where Mr. Keene kept his papers. I ought to have them in hand at once." Mrs. Keene remembered to press her handkerchief to her eyes, and Gordon hastily added, "Since Dr. Rigdon is gone, perhaps this lady—what is her name?—Geraldine—could save you the trouble."

"Mercy, yes!" she declared emphatically. "For I really do not know where to begin to look. Geraldine will know or guess. I'll go straight and rouse Geraldine out of bed."

She preceded Gordon into the hall, and, flinging over her shoulder the admonition, "Make yourself at home, I beg," ran lightly up the stairs.

Meantime Gordon strolled to the broad front door that stood open from morning to night, winter and summer, and paused there to light his cigar. All his characteristics were accented in the lustre of the vivid day, albeit for the most part they were of a null, negative tendency, for he had an inexpressive, impersonal manner and a sort of aloof, reserved dignity. His outward aspect

THE PHANTOM OF BOGUE HOLAUBA

seemed rather the affair of his up-to-date metropolitan tailor and barber than any exponent of his character and mind. He was not much beyond thirty years of age, and his straight, fine, dark hair was worn at the temples more by the fluctuations of stocks than the ravages of time. He was pale, of medium height, and slight of build; he listened with a grave, deliberate attention and an inscrutable gray eye, very steady, coolly observant, an appreciable asset in the brokerage business. He was all unaccustomed to the waste of time, and it was with no slight degree of impatience that he looked about him.

The magnolia grove filled the space to the half-seen gate in front of the house, but away on either side were long vistas. To the right the river was visible, and, being one of the great bends of the stream, it seemed to run directly to the west, the prospect only limited by the horizon line. On the other side, a glare, dazzlingly white in the sun, proclaimed the cotton-fields. Afar the gin-house showed, with its smoke-stack, like an obeliscal column, from which issued heavy coils of vapor, and occasionally came the raucous grating of a screw, telling that the baler was at work. Interspersed throughout the fields were the busy cotton-pickers, and now and again rose snatches of song as they heaped the great baskets in the turn-rows.

Within the purlieus of the inclosure about the mansion there was no stir of industry, no sign of life, save indeed an old hound lying on the veranda steps, looking up with great, liquid, sherry-tinted eyes at the stranger, and, though wheezing a wish to lick his hand, unable to muster the energy to rise.

After an interval of a few moments Gordon turned within. He felt that he must forthwith get at the papers and set this little matter in order. He paused baffled at the door of the parlor, where satin damask and rosewood furniture, lace curtains and drawn shades, held out no promise of repositories of business papers. On the opposite side of the hall was a sitting-room that bore evidence of constant use. Here was a desk of the old-fashioned kind, with a bookcase as a superstructure, and a writing-table stood in the centre of the floor, equipped with a number of drawers which were all locked, as a tentative touch soon told. He had not concluded its examination when a step and rustle behind him betokened a sudden entrance.

"Miss Geraldine Norris!" a voice broke upon the air,—a voice that he had not before heard, and he turned abruptly to greet the lady as she formally introduced herself.

A veritable Titania she seemed as she swayed in the doorway. She was a little thing, delicately built, slender yet not thin, with lustrous golden hair, large, well-opened, dark blue eyes, a complexion daintily white and roseate,—a fairy-like presence indeed, but with a prosaic, matter-of-fact manner and a dogmatic pose of laying down the law.

Gordon could never have imagined himself so disconcerted as when she advanced upon him with the caustic query, "Why did you not ask Mrs. Keene for her husband's keys? Surely that is simple enough!" She flung a bunch of keys on a steel ring down upon the table. "Heavens! to be roused from my well-earned slumbers at daybreak to solve this problem! 'Hurry! Hurry! Hurry!'" She mimicked Mrs. Keene's urgency, then broke out laughing.

"Now," she demanded, all unaffected by

his mien of surprised and offended dignity, "do you think yourself equal to the task of fitting these keys,—or shall I lend you my strong right arm?"

It is to be doubted if Gordon had ever experienced such open ridicule as when she came smiling up to the table, drawing back the sleeve of her gown from her delicate dimpled wrist. She wore a white dress, such as one never sees save in that Southern country, so softly sheer, falling in such graceful, floating lines, with a deep, plain hem and no touch of garniture save, perhaps, an edge of old lace on the surplice neck. The cut of the dress showed a triangular section of her soft white chest and all the firm modelling of her throat and chin. It was evidently not a new gown, for a rent in one of the sleeves had been sewed up somewhat too obviously, and there was a darn on the shoulder where a rose-bush had snagged the fabric. A belt of black velvet, with long, floating sash-ends, was about her waist, and a band of black velvet held in place her shining hair.

"I am sorry to have been the occasion of disturbing you," he said with stiff formality, "and I am very much obliged, certainly," he added, as he took up the keys.

THE PHANTOM OF BOGUE HOLAUBA

"I may consider myself dismissed from the presence?" she asked saucily. "Then, I will permit myself a cup of chocolate and a roll, and be ready for any further commands."

She frisked out of the door, and, frowning heavily, he sat down to the table and opened the top-drawer, which yielded instantly to the first key that he selected.

The first paper, too, on which he laid his hand was the will, signed and witnessed, regularly executed, all its provisions seeming, as he glanced through it, reasonable and feasible. As he laid it aside, he experienced the business man's satisfaction with a document duly capable of the ends desired. Then he opened with a sudden flicker of curiosity a bulky envelope placed with the will and addressed to himself. He read it through, the natural interest on his face succeeded by amazement, increasing gradually to fear, the chill drops starting from every pore. He had grown ghastly white before he had concluded the perusal, and for a long time he sat as motionless as if turned to stone.

The September day glowed outside in sumptuous splendor. A glad wind sprang up and sped afield. Geraldine, her breakfast finished, a broad hat canted down over her eyes, rushed through the hall as noisily as a boy, prodded up the old hound, and ran him a race around the semicircle of the drive. A trained hound he had been in his youth, and he was wont to conceal and deny certain ancient accomplishments. But even he realized that it was waste of breath to say nay to the persistent Geraldine. He resigned himself to go through all his repertoire,—was a dead dog, begged, leaped a stick back and forth, went lame, and in his newly awakened interest performed several tricks of which she had been unaware. Her joyful cries of commendation—"Played an encore! *an encore!* He did, he did! Cutest old dog in the United States!" caught Mrs. Keene's attention.

"Geraldine," she screamed from an upper window, "come in out of the sun! You will have a sun-stroke—and ruin your complexion besides! You know you ought to be helping that man with those papers,— he won't be able to do anything without you!" Her voice quavered on the last words, as if she suddenly realized "that man" might overhear her,—as indeed he did. But he made no sign. He sat still, stultified and

THE PHANTOM OF BOGUE HOLAUBA

stony, silently gazing at the paper in his hands.

When luncheon was announced, Gordon asked to have something light sent in to him, as he wished not to be disturbed in his investigation of the documents. He had scant need to apprehend interruption, however, while the long afternoon wore gradually away. The universal Southern siesta was on, and the somnolent mansion was like the castle of Sleeping Beauty. The ladies had sought their apartments and the downy couches; the cook, on a shady bench under the trellis, nodded as she seeded the raisins for the frozen pudding of the six-o'clock dinner; the waiter had succumbed in clearing the lunch-table and made mesmeric passes with the dish-rag in a fantasy of washing the plates; the stable-boy slumbered in the hay, high in the loft, while the fat old coachman, with a chamois-skin in his hand, dozed as he sat on the step of the surrey, between the fenders; the old dog snored on the veranda floor, and Mrs. Keene's special attendant, who was really more a seamstress than a ladies' maid, dreamed that for some mysterious reason she could not thread a needle to fashion in a vast hurry the second mourning of her employer, who she imagined would call for it within a week!

Outside the charmed precincts of this Castle Indolence, the busy cotton-pickers knew no pause nor stay. The steam-engine at the gin panted throughout all the long hot hours, the baler squealed and rasped and groaned, as it bound up the product into marketable compass, but there was no one waking near enough to note how the guest of the mansion was pacing the floor in a stress of nervous excitement, and to comment on the fact.

Toward sunset, a sudden commotion roused the slumbrous place. There had been an accident at the gin,—a boy had been caught in the machinery and variously mangled. Dr. George Rigdon had been called and had promptly sewed up the wounds. A runner had been sent to the mansion for bandages, brandy, fresh clothing, and sundry other collateral necessities of the surgery, and the news had thrown the house into unwonted excitement.

"The boy won't die, then?" Geraldine asked of a second messenger, as he stood by the steps of the veranda, waiting for the desired commodities.

"Lawdy,—*no,* ma'am! He is as good as new! Doc' George, *he* fix him up."

Gordon, whom the tumult had summoned forth from his absorptions, noted Geraldine's triumphant laugh as she received this report, the toss of her spirited little head, the light in her dark blue eyes, deepening to sapphire richness, her obvious pride in the skill, the humanitarian achievement, of her lover. Dr. George must be due here this evening, he fancied. For she was all freshly bedight; her gown was embellished with delicate laces, and its faint green hue gave her the aspect of some water-sprite, posed against that broad expanse of the Mississippi River, that was itself of a jade tint reflected from a green and amber sky; at the low horizon line the vermilion sun was sinking into its swirling depths.

Gordon perceived a personal opportunity in the prospect of this guest for the evening. He must have counsel, he was thinking. He could not act on his own responsibility in this emergency that had suddenly confronted him. He was still too overwhelmed by the strange experience he had encountered, too shaken. This physician was a man of intelligence, of skill in his chosen profession, necessarily a man worth while in many ways. He was an intimate friend of the Keene family, and might the more heartily lend a helping hand. The thought, the hope, cleared Gordon's brow, but still the impress of the stress of the afternoon was so marked that the girl was moved to comment in her brusque way as they stood together on the cool, fern-embowered veranda.

"Why, Mr. Gordon," she exclaimed in surprise, "you have no idea how strange you look! You must have overworked awfully this afternoon. Why, you look as if you had seen a ghost!"

To her amazement, he recoiled abruptly. Involuntarily, he passed his hand over his face, as if seeking to obliterate the traces she had deciphered. Then, with an obvious effort, he recovered a show of equanimity; he declared that it was only because he was so tousled in contrast with her fresh finery that she thought he looked supernaturally horrible! He would go upstairs forthwith and array himself anew.

THE PHANTOM OF BOGUE HOLAUBA

Gordon proved himself a true prophet, for Rigdon came to dine. With the postprandial cigars, the two gentlemen, at Gordon's suggestion, repaired to the sitting-room to smoke, instead of joining their hostess on the veranda, where tobacco was never interdicted. Indeed, they did not come forth thence for nearly two hours, and were palpably embarrassed when Geraldine declared in bewilderment, gazing at them in the lamplight that fell from within, through one of the great windows, that now *both* looked as if they had seen a ghost!

Despite their efforts to sustain the interest of the conversation, they were obviously distrait, and had a proclivity to fall into sudden silences, and Mrs. Keene found them amazingly unresponsive and dull. Thus it was that she rose as if to retire for the night while the hour was still early. In fact, she intended to utilize the opportunity to have some dresses of the first mourning outfit tried on, for which the patient maid was now awaiting her.

"I leave you a charming substitute," she said in making her excuses. "Geraldine need not come in yet—it is not late."

THE PHANTOM OF BOGUE HOLAUBA

Her withdrawal seemed to give a fresh impetus to some impulse with which Rigdon had been temporizing. He recurred to it at once. "You contemplate giving it to the public," he said to Gordon; "why not try its effect on a disinterested listener first, and judge from that?"

Gordon assented with an extreme gravity that surprised Geraldine; then Rigdon hesitated, evidently scarcely knowing how to begin. He looked vaguely at the moon riding high in the heavens above the long, broad expanse of the Mississippi and the darkling forests on either hand. Sometimes a shaft of light, a sudden luminous glister, betokened the motion of the currents gliding in the sheen. "Last night," he said in a tense, bated voice—"last night Mr. Gordon saw the phantom of Bogue Holauba. Stop! Hush!"—for the girl had sprung half screaming from her chair. "This is important." He laid his hand on her arm to detain her. "We want you to help us!"

"Help you! Why, you scare me to death!" She had paused, but stood trembling from head to foot.

"There is something explained in one of

Mr. Keene's papers,—addressed to Mr. Gordon; and we have been much startled by the coincidence of his—his vision."

"Did he see—really——?" Geraldine had sunk back in her chair, her face ghastly pale.

"Of course it must be some illusion," said Rigdon. "The effect of the mist, perhaps——"

"Only, there was no mist," said Gordon.

"Perhaps a snag waving in the wind."

"Only, there was no wind."

"Perhaps a snag tossing in the motion of the water,—at all events, you can't say there was no water." Dr. Rigdon glanced at Gordon with a genial smile.

"Mighty little water for the Mississippi," Gordon sought to respond in the same key.

"You know the record of these apparitions." Leaning forward, one arm on his knee, the document in question in his hand, Rigdon looked up into Geraldine's pale face. "In the old days there used to be a sort of water-gypsy, with a queer little trading-boat that plied the region of the bends—a queer little old man, too—Polish, I think, foreign certainly—and the butt of all the

THE PHANTOM OF BOGUE HOLAUBA

wags alongshore, at the stores and the woodyards, the cotton-sheds and the wharf-boats. By some accident, it was thought, the boat got away when he was befuddled with drink in a wood-chopper's cabin—a stout, trig little craft it was! When he found it was gone, he was wild, for although he saw it afloat at a considerable distance down the Mississippi, it suddenly disappeared near Bogue Holauba, cargo and all. No trace of its fate was ever discovered. He haunted these banks then—whatever he may have done since—screaming out his woes for his losses, and his rage and curses on the miscreants who had set the craft adrift—for he fully believed it was done in malice—beating his breast and tearing his hair. The Civil War came on presently, and the man was lost sight of in the national commotions. No one thought of him again till suddenly something—an apparition, an illusion, the semblance of a man—began to patrol the banks of Bogue Holauba, and beat its breast and tear its hair and bewail its woes in pantomime, and set the whole country-side aghast, for always disasters follow its return."

"And how do you account for that

phase?" asked Gordon, obviously steadying his voice by an effort of the will.

"The apparition always shows up at low water,—the disasters are usually typhoid," replied the physician.

"Mr. Keene died from malaria," Geraldine murmured musingly.

The two men glanced significantly at each other. Then Rigdon resumed: "I mustered the hardihood on one occasion to row up to the bank of Bogue Holauba for a closer survey. The thing vanished on my approach. There was a snag hard by, fast anchored in the bottom of the Bogue. It played slackly to and fro with the current, but I could not see any way by which it or its shadow could have produced the illusion."

"Is this what you had to tell me?" demanded Geraldine pertinently. "I knew all that already."

"No, no," replied the Doctor reluctantly. "Will you tell it, Mr. Gordon, or shall I?"

"You, by all means, if you will," said Gordon gloomily. "God knows I should be glad never to speak of it."

"Well," Rigdon began slowly, "Mr. Gordon was made by his cousin Jasper Keene not only the executor of his will, but the repository of a certain confession, which he may destroy or make public as he sees proper. It seems that in Mr. Keene's gay young days, running wild in his vacation from college on a secluded plantation, he often lacked congenial companionship, and he fell in with an uncouth fellow of a lower social grade, who led him into much detrimental adventure. Among other incidents of very poor fun, the two were notable in hectoring and guying the old Polish trader, who, when drunk on mean whisky as he often was, grew violent and antagonistic. He went very far in his denunciations one fatal night, and by way of playing him a trick in return, they set his boat adrift by cutting the rope that tied the craft to a tree on the bank. The confession states that they supposed the owner was then aboard and would suffer no greater hardship than having to use the sweeps with considerable energy to row her in to a landing again. They were genuinely horrified when he came running down the bank, both arms out-stretched, crying out that his all, *his all* was floating away on that tumultuous, merciless tide. Before any skiff could be

THE PHANTOM OF BOGUE HOLAUBA

launched, before any effort could be made to reach the trading-boat, she suddenly disappeared. The Mississippi was at flood height, and it was thought that the boat struck some drifting obstruction, swamped, and went down in deep water. The agents in this disaster were never suspected, but as soon as Jasper Keene had come of age, and had command of any means of his own, his first act was to have an exhaustive search made for the old fellow, with a view of financial restitution. But the owner of the trading-boat had died, spending his last years in the futile effort to obtain the insurance money. As the little he had left was never claimed, no representative could profit by the restitution that Jasper Keene had planned, and he found what satisfaction he could in giving it secretly to an old man's charity. Then the phantom began to take his revenge. He appeared on the banks of Bogue Holauba, and straightway the only child of the mansion sickened and died. Mr. Keene's first wife died after the second apparition. Either it was the fancy of an ailing man, or perhaps the general report, but he notes that the spectre was bewailing its woes along the banks of Bogue Holauba when Jasper Keene himself was stricken by an illness which from the first he felt was fatal."

"I remember—I remember it was said at the time," Geraldine barely whispered.

"And now to the question: he leaves it to Mr. Gordon as his kinsman, solicitous of the family repute, to judge whether this confession should be made public or destroyed."

"Does he state any reasons for making it public?" demanded Geraldine, taking the document and glancing through its pages.

"Yes; as an expiation of his early misdeeds toward this man and, if any such thing there be, to placate the spirit of his old enemy; and lastly better to secure his peace with his Maker."

"And which do you say?" Geraldine turned an eager, spirited face toward Gordon, his dejected attitude and countenance distinctly seen in the light from the lamp within the parlor, on a table close to the window.

"I frankly admit that the publication of that confession would humiliate me to the ground, but I fear that it *ought* to be given to the public, as he obviously desires!"

"And which do *you* say?" Geraldine was standing now, and swiftly whirled around toward Dr. Rigdon.

"I agree with Mr. Gordon—much against my will—but an honest confession is good for the soul!" he replied ruefully.

"You infidels!" she exclaimed tumultuously. "You have not one atom of Christian faith between you! To imagine that *you* can strike a bargain with the good God by letting a sick theory of expiation of a dying, fever-distraught creature besmirch his repute as a man and a gentleman, make his whole life seem like a whited sepulchre, and bring his name into odium,—as kind a man as ever lived,—and you know it!—as honest, and generous, and whole-souled, to be held up to scorn and humiliation because of a boyish prank forty years ago, that precipitated a disaster never intended,—bad enough, silly enough, even wicked enough, but not half so bad and silly and wicked as *you*, with your morbid shrinking from moral responsibility, and your ready contributive defamation of character. Tell me, you men, is this a testamentary paper, and you think it against the law to destroy it?"

THE PHANTOM OF BOGUE HOLAUBA

"No, no, not that," said Rigdon.

"No, it is wholly optional," declared Gordon.

"Then, I will settle the question for you once for all, you wobblers!" She suddenly thrust the paper into the chimney of the lamp on the table just within the open window, and as it flared up she flung the document forth, blazing in every fibre, on the bare driveway below the veranda. "And now you may find, as best you can, some other means of exorcising the phantom of Bogue Holauba!"

HIS CHRISTMAS MIRACLE

He yearned for a sign from the heavens. Could one intimation be vouchsafed him, how it would confirm his faltering faith! Jubal Kennedy was of the temperament impervious to spiritual subtleties, fain to reach conclusions with the line and rule of mathematical demonstration. Thus, all unreceptive, he looked through the mountain gap, as through some stupendous gateway, on the splendors of autumn; the vast landscape glamorous in a transparent amethystine haze; the foliage of the dense primeval wilderness in the October richness of red and russet; the " hunter's moon," a full sphere of illuminated pearl, high in the blue east while yet the dull vermilion sun swung westering above the massive purple heights. He knew how the sap was sinking; that the growths of the year had now failed; presently all would be shrouded in snow, but only to rise again in the reassurance of vernal quickening, to glow anew in the fullness of bloom, to attain eventually the perfection of fruition. And still he was deaf to the reiterated analogy of death, and blind to the immanent obvious prophecy of resurrection and the life to come.

His thoughts, as he stood on this jutting crag in Sunrise Gap, were with a recent "experience meeting" at which he had sought to canvass his spiritual needs. His demand of a sign from the heavens as evidence of the existence of the God of revelation, as assurance of the awakening of divine grace in the human heart, as actual proof that wistful mortality is inherently endowed with immortality, had electrified this symposium. Though it was fashionable, so to speak, in this remote cove among the Great Smoky Mountains, to be repentant in rhetorical involutions and a self-accuser in finespun interpretations of sin, doubt, or more properly an eager questioning, a desire to possess the sacred mysteries of religion, was unprecedented. Kennedy was a proud man, reticent, reserved. Although the old parson, visibly surprised and startled, had gently invited his full confidence, Kennedy had hastily swallowed his words, as best he might, perceiving that the congregation had wholly misinterpreted their true intent and that cer-

HIS CHRISTMAS MIRACLE

tain gossips had an unholy relish of the sensation they had caused.

Thereafter he indulged his poignant longings for the elucidation of the veiled truths only when, as now, he wandered deep in the woods with his rifle on his shoulder. He could not have said to-day that he was nearer an inspiration, a hope, a "leading," than heretofore, but as he stood on the crag it was with the effect of a dislocation that he was torn from the solemn theme by an interruption at a vital crisis.

The faint vibrations of a violin stirred the reverent hush of the landscape in the blended light of the setting sun and the "hunter's moon." Presently the musician came into view, advancing slowly through the aisles of the red autumn forest. A rapt figure it was, swaying in responsive ecstasy with the rhythmic cadence. The head, with its long, blowsy yellow hair, was bowed over the dark polished wood of the instrument; the eyes were half closed; the right arm, despite the eccentric patches on the sleeve of the old brown-jeans coat, moved with free, elastic gestures in all the liberties of a practiced bowing. If he saw the hunter motionless on the brink of the crag, the fiddler gave no intimation. His every faculty was as if enthralled by the swinging iteration of the sweet melancholy melody, rendered with a breadth of effect, an inspiration, it might almost have seemed, incongruous with the infirmities of the crazy old fiddle. He was like a creature under the sway of a spell, and apparently drawn by this dulcet lure of the enchantment of sound was the odd procession that trailed silently after him through these deep mountain fastnesses.

A woman came first, arrayed in a ragged purple skirt and a yellow blouse open at the throat, displaying a slender white neck which upheld a face of pensive, inert beauty. She clasped in her arms a delicate infant, ethereal of aspect with its flaxen hair, transparently pallid complexion, and wide blue eyes. It was absolutely quiescent, save that now and then it turned feebly in its waxen hands a little striped red-and-yellow pomegranate. A sturdy blond toddler trudged behind, in a checked blue cotton frock, short enough to disclose cherubic pink feet and legs bare to the knee; he carried that treasure of rural

HIS CHRISTMAS MIRACLE

juveniles, a cornstalk violin. An old hound, his tail suavely wagging, padded along the narrow path; and last of all came, with frequent pause to crop the wayside herbage, a large cow, brindled red and white.

"The whole fambly!" muttered Kennedy. Then, aloud, "Why don't you uns kerry the baby, Basil Bedell, an' give yer wife a rest?"

At the prosaic suggestion the crystal realm of dreams was shattered. The bow, with a quavering discordant scrape upon the strings, paused. Then Bedell slowly mastered the meaning of the interruption.

"Kerry the baby? Why, Aurely won't let none but herself tech that baby." He laughed as he tossed the tousled yellow hair from his face, and looked over his shoulder to speak to the infant. "It air sech a plumb special delightsome peach, it air,—it air!"

The pale face of the child lighted up with a smile of recognition and a faint gleam of mirth.

"I jes' kem out ennyhows ter drive up the cow," Basil added.

"Big job," sneered Kennedy. " 'Pearslike it takes the whole fambly to do it."

Such slothful mismanagement was calculated to affront an energetic spirit. Obviously, at this hour the woman should be at home cooking the supper.

"I follered along ter listen ter the fiddle, —ef ye hev enny call ter know." Mrs. Bedell replied to his unspoken thought, as if by divination.

But indeed such strictures were not heard for the first time. They were in some sort the penalty of the disinterested friendship which Kennedy had harbored for Basil since their childhood. He wished that his compeer might prosper in such simple wise as his own experience had proved to be amply possible. Kennedy's earlier incentive to industry had been his intention to marry, but the object of his affections had found him "too mortal solemn," and without a word of warning had married another man in a distant cove. The element of treachery in this event had gone far to reconcile the jilted lover to his future, bereft of her companionship, but the habit of industry thus formed had continued of its own momentum. It had resulted in forehanded thrift; he now possessed a comfortable holding,—cattle, house, ample land; and he had all the intolerance of the ant for the cricket. As Bedell lifted the bow once more, every wincing nerve was enlisted in arresting it in mid-air.

"Mighty long tramp fur Bobbie, thar,—why n't ye kerry him?"

The imperturbable calm still held fast on the musician's face. "Bob," he addressed the toddler, "will you uns let daddy kerry ye like a baby?"

He swooped down as if to lift the child, the violin and bow in his left hand. The hardy youngster backed off precipitately.

"Don't ye *dare* ter do it!" he virulently admonished his parent, a resentful light in his blue eyes. Then, as Bedell sang a stave in a full rich voice, "Bye-oh, Baby!" Bob vociferated anew, "Don't you *begin* ter dare do it!" every inch a man though a little one.

"That's the kind of a fambly I hev got," Basil commented easily. "Wife an' boy an' baby all walk over me,—plumb stomp on me! Jes' enough lef' of me ter play the fiddle a leetle once in a while."

"Mighty nigh all the while, I be afeared," Kennedy corrected the phrase. "How did

HIS CHRISTMAS MIRACLE

yer corn crap turn out?" he asked, as he too fell into line and the procession moved on once more along the narrow path.

"Well enough," said Basil; "we uns hev got a sufficiency." Then, as if afraid of seeming boastful he qualified, "Ye know I hain't got but one muel ter feed, an' the cow thar. My sheep gits thar pastur' on the volunteer grass 'mongst the rocks, an' I hev jes' got a few head ennyhows."

"But *why* hain't ye got more, Basil? Why n't ye work more and quit wastin' yer time on that old fool fiddle?"

The limits of patience were reached. The musician fired up. " 'Kase," he retorted, "I make enough. I hev got grace enough ter be thankful fur sech ez be vouchsafed ter me. *I* ain't wantin' no meracle."

Kennedy flushed, following in silence while the musician annotated his triumph by a series of gay little harmonics, and young Hopeful, trudging in the rear, executed a soundless fantasia on the cornstalk fiddle with great brilliancy of technique.

"You uns air talkin' 'bout whut I said at the meetin' las' month," Kennedy observed at length.

HIS CHRISTMAS MIRACLE

"An' so be all the mounting," Aurelia interpolated with a sudden fierce joy of reproof.

Kennedy winced visibly.

"The folks all 'low ez ye be no better than an onbeliever." Aurelia was bent on driving the blade home. "The idee of axin' fur a meracle at this late day,—so ez *ye* kin be satisfied in yer mind ez ye hev got grace! Providence, though merciful, air *obleeged,* ter know ez sech air plumb scandalous an' redic'lous."

"Why, Aurely, hesh up," exclaimed her husband, startled from his wonted leniency. "I hev never hearn ye talk in sech a key,— yer voice sounds plumb out o' tune. I be plumb sorry, Jube, ez I spoke ter you uns 'bout a meracle at all. But I war consider'ble nettled by yer words, ye see,—'kase I know I be a powerful, lazy, shif'less cuss——"

"Ye know a lie, then," his helpmate interrupted promptly.

"Why, Aurely, hesh up,—ye—ye—*woman,* ye!" he concluded injuriously. Then resuming his remarks to Kennedy, "I know I *do* fool away a deal of my time with the fiddle——"

"The sound of it is like bread ter me,—

HIS CHRISTMAS MIRACLE

I couldn't live without it," interposed the unconquered Aurelia. "Sometimes it minds me o' the singin' o' runnin' water in a lonesome place. Then agin it minds me o' seein' sunshine in a dream. An' sometimes it be sweet an' high an' fur off, like a voice from the sky, tellin' what no mortial ever knowed before,—an' *then* it minds me o' the tune them angels sung ter the shepherds abidin' in the fields. I *couldn't* live without it."

"Woman, hold yer jaw!" Basil proclaimed comprehensively. Then, renewing his explanation to Kennedy, "I kin see that I don't purvide fur my fambly ez I ought ter do, through hatin' work and lovin' to play the fiddle."

"I ain't goin' ter hear my home an' hearth reviled." Aurelia laid an imperative hand on her husband's arm. "Ye know ye couldn't make more out'n sech ground,—though I ain't faultin' our land, neither. We uns hev enough an' ter spare, all we need an' more than we deserve. We don't need ter ax a meracle from the skies ter stay our souls on faith, nor a sign ter prove our grace."

"Now, now, *stop,* Aurely!—I declar', Jube I dunno what made me lay my tongue ter sech

HIS CHRISTMAS MIRACLE

a word ez that thar miser'ble benighted meracle! I be powerful sorry I hurt yer feelin's, Jube; folks seekin' salvation git mightily mis-put sometimes, an'——"

"I don't want ter hear none o' yer views on religion," Kennedy interrupted gruffly. An apology often augments the sense of injury. In this instance it also annulled the provocation, for his own admission put Bedell hopelessly in the wrong. "Ez a friend I war argufyin' with ye agin' yer waste o' time with that old fool fiddle. Ye hev got wife an' children, an' yit not so well off in this world's gear ez me, a single man. I misdoubts ef ye hev hunted a day since the craps war laid by, or hev got a pound o' jerked venison stored up fer winter. But this air yer home,"—he pointed upward at a little clearing beginning, as they approached, to be visible amidst the forest,—"an' ef ye air satisfied with sech ez it be, that comes from laziness stiddier a contented sperit."

With this caustic saying he suddenly left them, the procession standing silently staring after him as he took his way through the woods in the dusky red shadows of the autumnal gloaming.

HIS CHRISTMAS MIRACLE

Aurelia's vaunted home was indeed a poor place,—not even the rude though substantial log-cabin common to the region. It was a flimsy shanty of boards, and except for its rickety porch was more like a box than a house. It had its perch on a jutting eminence, where it seemed the familiar of the skies, so did the clouds and winds circle about it. Through the great gateway of Sunrise Gap it commanded a landscape of a scope that might typify a world, in its multitude of mountain ranges, in the intricacies of its intervening valleys, in the glittering coils of its water-courses. Basil would sometimes sink into deep silences, overpowered by the majesty of nature in this place. After a long hiatus the bow would tremble and falter on the strings as if overawed for a time; presently the theme would strengthen, expand, resound with large meaning, and then he would send forth melodies that he had never before played or heard, his own dream, the reflection of that mighty mood of nature in the limpid pool of his receptive mind.

Around were rocks, crags, chasms,—the fields which nourished the family lay well from the verge, within the purlieus of the

HIS CHRISTMAS MIRACLE

limited mountain plateau. He had sought to persuade himself that it was to save all the arable land for tillage that he had placed his house and door-yard here, but both he and Aurelia were secretly aware of the subterfuge; he would fain be always within the glamour of the prospect through Sunrise Gap!

Their interlocutor had truly deemed that the woman should have been earlier at home cooking the supper. Dusk had deepened to darkness long before the meal smoked upon the board. The spinning-wheel had begun to whir for her evening stint when other hillfolks had betaken themselves to bed. Basil puffed his pipe before the fire; the flicker and flare pervaded every nook of the bright little house. Strings of red-pepper-pods flaunted in festoons from the beams; the baby slumbered under a gay quilt in his rude cradle, never far from his mother's hand, but the bluff little boy was still up and about, although his aspect, round and burly, in a scanty nightgown, gave token of recognition of the fact that bed was his appropriate place. His shrill plaintive voice rose ever and anon wakefully.

HIS CHRISTMAS MIRACLE

"I wanter hear a bear tale,—I wanter hear a bear tale."

Thus Basil must needs knock the ashes from his pipe the better to devote himself to the narration,—a prince of raconteurs, to judge by the spell-bound interest of the youngster who stood at his knee and hung on his words. Even Aurelia checked the whir of her wheel to listen smilingly. She broke out laughing in appreciative pleasure when Basil took up the violin to show how a jovial old bear, who intruded into this very house one day when all the family were away at the church in the cove, and who mistook the instrument for a banjo, addressed himself to picking out this tune, singing the while a quaint and ursine lay. Basil embellished the imitation with a masterly effect of realistic growls.

"Ef ye keep goin' at that gait, Basil," Aurelia admonished him, "daylight will ketch us all wide awake around the fire,—no wonder the child won't go to bed." She seemed suddenly impressed with the pervasive cheer. "What a fool that man, Jube Kennedy, must be! How *could* ennybody hev a sweeter, darlinger home than we uns hev got hyar in Sunrise Gap!"

HIS CHRISTMAS MIRACLE

On the languorous autumn a fierce winter ensued. The cold came early. The deciduous growths of the forests were leafless ere November waned, rifled by the riotous marauding winds. December set in with the gusty snow flying fast. Drear were the gray skies; ghastly the sheeted ranges. Drifts piled high in bleak ravines, and the grim gneissoid crags were begirt with gigantic icicles. But about the little house in Sunrise Gap that kept so warm a heart, the holly trees showed their glad green leaves and the red berries glowed with a mystic significance.

As the weeks wore on, the place was often in Kennedy's mind, although he had not seen it since that autumn afternoon when he had bestirred himself to rebuke its owner concerning the inadequacies of the domestic provision. His admonition had been kindly meant and had not deserved the retort, the flippant ridicule of his spiritual yearnings. Though he still winced from the recollection, he was sorry that he had resisted the importunacy of Basil's apology. He realized that Aurelia had persisted to the limit of her power in the embitterment of the controversy, but even Aurelia he was disposed to forgive as time passed on. When Christmas

HIS CHRISTMAS MIRACLE

Day dawned, the vague sentiment began to assume the definiteness of a purpose, and noontide found him on his way to Sunrise Gap.

There was now no path through the woods; the snow lay deep over all, unbroken save at long intervals when queer footprints gave token of the stirring abroad of the sylvan denizens, and he felt an idle interest in distinguishing the steps of wolf and fox, of opossum and weasel. In the intricacies of the forest aisles, amid laden boughs of pine and fir, there was a suggestion of darkness, but all the sky held not enough light to cast the shadow of a bole on the white blank spaces of the snow-covered ground. A vague blue haze clothed the air; yet as he drew near the mountain brink, all was distinct in the vast landscape, the massive ranges and alternating valleys in infinite repetition.

He wondered when near the house that he had not heard the familiar barking of the old hound; then he remembered that the sound of his horse's hoofs was muffled by the snow. He was glad to be unheralded. He would like to surprise Aurelia into geniality before her vicarious rancor for Basil's sake should

HIS CHRISTMAS MIRACLE

be roused anew. As he emerged from the thick growths of the holly, with the icy scintillations of its clustering green leaves and red berries, he drew rein so suddenly that the horse was thrown back on his haunches. The rider sat as if petrified in the presence of an awful disaster.

The house was gone! Even the site had vanished! Kennedy stared bewildered. Slowly the realization of what had chanced here began to creep through his brain. Evidently there had been a gigantic landslide. The cliff-like projection was broken sheer off,—hurled into the depths of the valley. Some action of subterranean waters, throughout ages, doubtless, had been undermining the great crags till the rocky crust of the earth had collapsed. He could see even now how the freeze had fractured outcropping ledges where the ice had gathered in the fissures. A deep abyss that he remembered as being at a considerable distance from the mountain's brink, once spanned by a foot-bridge, now showed the remnant of its jagged, shattered walls at the extreme verge of the precipice.

A cold chill of horror benumbed his

senses. Basil, the wife, the children,—where were they? A terrible death, surely, to be torn from the warm securities of the hearth-stone, without a moment's warning, and hurled into the midst of this frantic turmoil of nature, down to the depths of the gap,—a thousand feet below! And at what time had this dread fate befallen his friend? He remembered that at the cross-roads' store, when he had paused on his way to warm himself that morning, some gossip was detailing the phenomenon of unseasonable thunder during the previous night, while others protested that it must have been only the clamors of "Christmas guns" firing all along the country-side. "A turrible cláp, it was," the raconteur had persisted. "Sounded ez ef all creation hed split apart." Perhaps, therefore, the catastrophe might be recent. Kennedy could scarcely command his muscles as he dismounted and made his way slowly and cautiously to the verge.

Any deviation from the accustomed routine of nature has an unnerving effect, unparalleled by disaster in other sort; no individual danger or doom, the aspect of death by drowning, or gunshot, or disease,

HIS CHRISTMAS MIRACLE

can so abash the reason and stultify normal expectation. Kennedy was scarcely conscious that he saw the vast disorder of the landslide, scattered from the precipice on the mountain's brink to the depths of the Gap—inverted roots of great pines thrust out in mid-air, foundations of crags riven asunder and hurled in monstrous fragments along the steep slant, unknown streams newly liberated from the caverns of the range and cascading from the crevices of the rocks. In effect he could not believe his own eyes. His mind realized the perception of his senses only when his heart suddenly plunged with a wild hope,—he had discerned amongst the turmoil a shape of line and rule, the little box-like hut! Caught as it was in the boughs of a cluster of pines and firs, uprooted and thrust out at an incline a little less than vertical, the inmates might have been spared such shock of the fall as would otherwise have proved fatal. Had the house been one of the substantial log-cabins of the region its timbers must have been torn one from another, the daubing and chinking scattered as mere atoms. But the more flimsy character of the little dwelling

HIS CHRISTMAS MIRACLE

had thus far served to save it,—the interdependent "framing" of its structure held fast; the upright studding and boards, nailed stoutly on, rendered it indeed the box that it looked. It was, so to speak, built in one piece, and no part was subjected to greater strain than another. But should the earth cave anew, should the tough fibres of one of those gigantic roots tear out from the loosened friable soil, should the elastic supporting branches barely sway in some errant gust of wind, the little box would fall hundreds of feet, cracked like a nut, shattering against the rocks of the levels below.

He wondered if the inmates yet lived,— he pitied them still more if they only existed to realize their peril, to await in an anguish of fear their ultimate doom. Perhaps—he felt he was but trifling with despair—some rescue might be devised.

Such a weird cry he set up on the brink of the mountain!—full of horror, grief, and that poignant hope. The echoes of the Gap seemed reluctant to repeat the tones, dull, slow, muffled in snow. But a sturdy halloo responded from the window, uppermost now, for the house lay on its side amongst the boughs. Kennedy thought he saw the pallid simulacrum of a face.

"This be Jube Kennedy," he cried, reassuringly. "I be goin' ter fetch help,—men, ropes, and a windlass."

"Make haste then,—we uns be nigh friz."

"Ye air in no danger of fire, then?" asked the practical man.

"We hev hed none,—before we war flunged off'n the bluff we hed squinched the fire ter pledjure Bob, ez he war afeard Santy Claus would scorch his feet comin' down the chimbley,—powerful lucky fur we uns; the fire would hev burnt the house bodaciously."

Kennedy hardly stayed to hear. He was off in a moment, galloping at frantic speed along the snowy trail scarcely traceable in the sad light of the gray day; taking short cuts through the densities of the laurel; torn by jagged rocks and tangles of thorny growths and broken branches of great trees; plunging now and again into deep drifts above concealed icy chasms, and rescuing with inexpressible difficulty the floundering, struggling horse; reaching again the open sheeted roadway, bruised, bleeding, exhausted, yet furiously plunging forward, rousing the sparsely settled country-side with imperative insistence for help in this matter of life or death!

Death, indeed, only,—for the enterprise was pronounced impossible by those more experienced than Kennedy. Among the men now on the bluff were several who had been employed in the silver mines of this region, and they demonstrated conclusively that a rope could not be worked clear of the obstructions of the face of the rugged and shattered cliffs; that a human being, drawn from the cabin, strapped in a chair, must needs be torn from it and flung into the abyss below, or beaten to a frightful death against the jagged rocks in the transit.

"But not ef the chair war ter be steadied by a guy-rope from say—from that thar old pine tree over thar," Kennedy insisted, indicating the long bole of a partially uprooted and inverted tree on the steeps. "The chair would swing cl'ar of the bluff then."

"But, Jube, it is onpossible ter git a guy-rope over ter that tree,—more than a man's life is wuth ter try it."

A moment ensued of absolute silence,—space, however, for a hard-fought battle.

HIS CHRISTMAS MIRACLE

The aspect of that mad world below, with every condition of creation reversed; a mistake in the adjustment of the winch and gear by the excited, reluctant, disapproving men; an overstrain on the fibres of the long-used rope; a slip on the treacherous ice; the dizzy whirl of the senses that even a glance downward at those drear depths set astir in the brain,—all were canvassed within his mental processes, all were duly realized in their entirety ere he said with a spare dull voice and dry lips,—

"Fix ter let me down ter that thar leanin' pine, boys,—I'll kerry a guy-rope over thar."

At one side the crag beetled, and although it was impossible thence to reach the cabin with a rope it would swing clear of obstructions here, and might bring the rescuer within touch of the pine, where could be fastened the guy-rope; the other end would be affixed to the chair which could be lowered to the cabin only from the rugged face of the cliff. Kennedy harbored no self-deception; he more than doubted the outcome of the enterprise. He quaked and turned pale with dread as with the great rope knotted about his arm-pits and around his waist he was swung over the brink at the point where the crag jutted forth,—lower and lower still; now nearing the slanting inverted pine, caught amidst the débris of earth and rock; now failing to reach its boughs; once more swinging back to a great distance, so did the length of the rope increase the scope of the pendulum; now nearing the pine again, and at last fairly lodged on the icy bole, knotting and coiling about it the end of the guy-rope, on which he had come and on which he must needs return.

It seemed, through the inexpert handling of the little group, a long time before the stout arm-chair was secured to the cables, slowly lowered, and landed at last on the outside of the hut. Many an anxious glance was cast at the slate-gray sky. An inopportune flurry of snow, a flaw of wind,—and even now all would be lost. Dusk too impended, and as the rope began to coil on the windlass at the signal to hoist every eye was strained to discern the identity of the first voyagers in this aërial journey,—the two children, securely lashed to the chair. This was well,—all felt that both parents might best wait, might risk the added delay. The chair came swinging easily, swiftly, along

HIS CHRISTMAS MIRACLE

the gradations of the rise, the guy-rope holding it well from the chances of contact with the jagged projections of the face of the cliff, and the first shout of triumph rang sonorously from the summit.

When next the chair rested on the cabin beside the window, a thrill of anxiety and anger went through Kennedy's heart to note, from his perch on the leaning pine, a struggle between husband and wife as to who should go first. Each was eager to take the many risks incident to the long wait in this precarious lodgment. The man was the stronger. Aurelia was forced into the chair, tied fast, pushed off, waving her hand to her husband, shedding floods of tears, looking at him for the last time, as she fancied, and calling out dismally, "Far'well, Basil, far'well."

Even this lugubrious demonstration could not damp the spirits of the men working like mad at the windlass. They were jovial enough for bursts of laughter when it became apparent that Basil had utilized the ensuing interval to tie together, in preparation for the ascent with himself, the two objects which he next most treasured, his violin and his old hound. The trusty chair bore all aloft,

HIS CHRISTMAS MIRACLE

and Basil was received with welcoming acclamations.

Before the rope was wound anew and for the last time, the aspect of the group on the cliff had changed. It had grown eerie, indistinct. The pines and firs showed no longer their sempervirent green, but were black amid the white tufted lines on their branches, that still served to accentuate their symmetry. The vale had disappeared in a sinister abyss of gloom, though Kennedy would not look down at its menace, but upward, always upward. Thus he saw, like some radiant and splendid star, the first torch whitely aglow on the brink of the precipice. It opened long avenues of light adown the snowy landscape,—soft blue shadows trailed after it, like half-descried draperies of elusive hovering beings. Soon the torch was duplicated; another and then another began to glow. Now several drew together, and like a constellation glimmered crownlike on the brow of the night, as he felt the rope stir with the signal to hoist.

Upward, always upward, his eyes on that radiant stellular coronal, as it shone white and splendid in the snowy night. And now it had lost its mystic glamour,—disintegrated by gradual approach he could see the long handles of the pine-knots; the red verges of the flame; the blue and yellow tones of the focus; the trailing wreaths of dun-tinted smoke that rose from them. Then became visible the faces of the men who held them, all crowding eagerly to the verge. But it was in a solemn silence that he was received; a drear cold darkness, every torch being struck downward into the snow; a frantic haste in unharnessing him from the ropes, for he was almost frozen. He was hardly apt enough to interpret this as an emotion too deep for words, but now and again, as he was disentangled, he felt about his shoulders a furtive hug, and more than one pair of the ministering hands must needs pause to wring his own hands hard. They practically carried him to a fire that had been built in a sheltered place in one of those grottoes of the region, locally called "Rock-houses." Its cavernous portal gave upon a dark interior, and not until they had turned a corner in a tunnel-like passage was revealed an arched space in a rayonnant suffusion of light, the fire itself obscured by the figures about it. His eyes were caught first by the aspect of a youthful

HIS CHRISTMAS MIRACLE

mother with a golden-haired babe on her breast; close by showed the head and horns of a cow; the mule was mercifully sheltered too, and stood near, munching his fodder; a cluster of sheep pressed after the steps of half a dozen men, that somehow in the clare-obscure reminded him of the shepherds of old summoned by good tidings of great joy.

A sudden figure started up with streaming white hair and patriarchal beard.

"Will ye deny ez ye hev hed a sign from the heavens, Jubal Kennedy?" the old circuit-rider straitly demanded. "How could ye hev strengthened yer heart fur sech a deed onless the grace o' God prevailed mightily within ye? Inasmuch as ye hev done it unto one o' the least o' these my brethren, ye hev done it unto me."

"That ain't the *kind* o' sign, parson," Kennedy faltered. "I be lookin' fur a meracle in the yearth or in the air, that I kin view or hear."

"The kingdom o' Christ is a spiritual kingdom," said the parson solemnly. "The kingdom o' Christ is a *spiritual* kingdom, an' great are the wonders that are wrought therein."